Also in the

series:

Canyon Chaos

Arctic Adventure

Desert Disaster

With special thanks
to Dan Metcalf

First published in 2013 by Curious Fox,
an imprint of Capstone Global Library Limited,
7 Pilgrim Street, London, EC4V 6LB
Registered company number: 6695582

www.curious-fox.com

Text © Hothouse Fiction Ltd 2013

Series created by Hothouse Fiction
www.hothousefiction.com

The author's moral rights are hereby asserted.

Cover illustration by Spooky Pooka
Cover design by Mandy Norman

ISBN 978 1 78202 049 3

1 3 5 7 9 10 8 6 4 2

A CIP catalogue for this book is available from the British Library.

Typeset in Avenir by Hothouse Fiction Ltd

Printed and bound in the United Kingdom by CPI Group (UK) Ltd, Croydon, CR0 4YY

MIX
Paper from
responsible sources
FSC® C020471

To Charlie and Issac Metcalf, my champions

CHAPTER ONE
Highlights and Heroes

"Come on, Cabbie! You can do it!" shouted Jimmy at the top of his voice. Cabbie squealed around a corner, his back end swerving away from the road. He was going so fast he nearly toppled over the side of the narrow track into the deep canyon below. The wheels span as the robot racer tried to speed off, sending a cloud of dust up into the air.

"Well, hot dawg! If that ain't the slyest, smartest bit of driving I seen in years!" said the American commentator on the TV.

Jimmy smiled proudly. "Watch your speed, Cabbie!" he shouted at the old, flickering television.

Of course, he had no reason to worry. He knew exactly what would happen next in the race – he had been driving Cabbie at the time.

Jimmy and his best friend Max were sat on the mouldy old sofa in Jimmy's living room, watching a re-run of the first stage of the Robot Races Championship. On the screen the plume of dust and exhaust smoke settled to show Cabbie racing along the sandy track, a heat haze rising in front of him. The camera rose to show the other contestants.

There was Princess Kako in her silver leathers, riding her robobike, Lightning. She looked effortlessly cool as she zipped along the track.

Chip, the American racer, was next in his large yellow digger-like robot called Dug. The size and weight of Dug meant that he didn't look as elegant as Princess Kako, more like a terrifying herd of buffalo stampeding down the track.

In his deadly-looking hoverbot Maximus, Samir – the quiet Egyptian boy – swept by as smoothly as a skater across an ice rink.

Missy, the Australian tomboy, trundled along in her four-wheeled giant racer, Monster.

Finally the camera panned to show the sleek black racing-car like robot named Zoom, and Jimmy winced as the camera turned to its driver, Horace Pelly. Horace had been annoying enough when Jimmy was at school with him, but now they were racing against each other, he had hit new levels of smugness. Jimmy couldn't believe it when Horace flipped the visor up on his helmet and winked at the camera, his gleaming white teeth reflecting in the sunlight before he accelerated off down the track.

Jimmy rolled his eyes at Horace. *What a show off*, he thought.

On the TV the racers were coming to the final section of the track and Jimmy allowed himself a grin. After all, he knew how the race ended!

"This is shaping up to be one of the most exciting finishes of a Robot Race ever!" bellowed the TV commentator.

"Go, Cabbie, go!" Max whooped in the living room, bouncing up and down on the sofa like a jack-in-the-box.

Jimmy watched as he saw himself and his rickety robot Cabbie closing in on the two state-of-the-art robots, Lightning and Zoom.

Jimmy had been watching the Robot Races for years and he still couldn't believe that now he was actually taking part in them. Even though he knew how it all turned out, he couldn't help feeling nervous as he watched himself speed down the home straight. With the finish line in sight, Princess Kako had opened up a gap between herself and the other two racers, leaving Jimmy and Horace battling it out for second place.

"Fire your rocket-boosters!" Max shouted at the TV, and Jimmy grinned. It was so strange to hear his best friend cheering him on in the same way that they'd always cheered for their favourite robot racers.

On the flickering screen, the other Jimmy held his nerve, waiting until the last moment to use his boosters. With the chequered flag in the air just a few hundred metres away, there was an explosion of fire from Cabbie's thrusters. The rockets propelled him across the line into second place.

"Yes!" yelled Jimmy.

"Awesome!" shrieked Max.

They leaped up in the air and high-fived before

doing a little jig together in the middle of the room. Jimmy immediately felt a bit silly celebrating a finish which had taken place over a week ago, but the re-run was the first chance he'd had to see the race since he'd taken part in it. The TV cut to the commentators in the studio.

"Well, I'll be...! It don't get more exciting than that! Princess Kako rockets into first place, while underdog Jimmy Roberts from" – the presenter paused while he tried to say the name of Jimmy's town – "Smed-ing-ham in the UK, takes second. A fine performance, and we're not the only ones who think so!"

The TV cut to a familiar face. Big Al, one of the superstars of Robot Races, stood alongside his robot, Crusher. He was Jimmy and Max's favourite ever contender. Jimmy had posters of Big Al all over his bedroom walls. Max was an even bigger fan. He had once asked his mum if he could get a tattoo of Crusher.

"Big Al, when it was announced that Lord Leadpipe was going to run the Robot Races Championship for children under sixteen years old, did you ever think the talent would be this good?" the interviewer asked.

The large American racer laughed – a big, booming laugh that shook Jimmy's old TV so hard that the picture frame on top of it slid off and crashed to the floor.

"We all know that Lord Leadpipe likes to shake things up, and he's a smart guy. He knew what he was doing! The racing I've seen from these youngsters has been *crazy*, man! That first race was amazing!" Big Al said, almost spitting out his gum in excitement.

"Who stood out for you?" asked the interviewer.

Big Al turned to look at the camera. "Folks, you only need to remember one name in this competition, and that's Jimmy Roberts."

Jimmy's mouth fell open as he heard his name being mentioned by one of his heroes.

"Jimmy's got it all – speed, style and timing. His racing last week was outstanding!"

Back home, Jimmy could barely breathe with shock. A little bit of dribble left his mouth and plopped onto the carpet.

"The robots this year are great," continued Big Al. "There are some sweet designs out there, but Cabbie's the one to watch. He reminds me of Crusher years ago when I first built him. He doesn't look all that great, but he's got *soul*."

Max jumped up and down on the sofa in excitement, his floppy brown hair swishing in different directions. "Big Al is a fan of *my* best friend. That practically makes him *my* friend! Jimmy, do you think he'd take us for a spin in Crusher?"

But Jimmy was too speechless to reply. He felt like he was in a dream. It was just a few weeks since he had first heard of the special Robot Races Championship for children. And on that very same day he'd learned that his eccentric old grandpa who drove a taxi for a living was actually a robotics genius. Within days Grandpa had knocked together a robot racer made out of his old taxi and some spare parts he had lying around in his shed. The next thing Jimmy knew, he was in the local time trials, and when he sped to victory, he became a contender for the championship. He was whisked off to the Grand Canyon to compete against the best young racers in the world.

Sometimes it felt so awesome that Jimmy thought he might explode.

"Well, I suppose I better get home," Max said.

"Mum wants to take me and my nan to the shops."

"Sounds like fun," Jimmy replied, pulling a face as he opened the front door.

"Not really," said Max. "I'll have to spend an hour watching them choose a pair of woolly socks. It's nowhere near as much fun as hanging around with your grandpa."

Jimmy grinned. Max was right: living with Grandpa *was* pretty cool. He watched Max trudge off down the street, then went and peered out of the back window. At the bottom of the garden was a rickety old wooden shed with small dirty windows. It looked like the kind of building that you would use for storing a lawnmower and maybe a couple of spades, but Jimmy knew that behind those doors lay the entrance to his grandpa's secret underground laboratory. It had been built by the most secret department of the Secret Services, and it was where Grandpa had built the world's first-ever robot...

The loud banging continued, followed by some horrible grinding and scraping noises. Grandpa had been down there ever since the previous day, when it had been announced on TV that the next race would be held in South America – a stage that the commentators were already calling "The Rainforest Rampage".

As Jimmy looked at the shed, sparks came flying out of the open window, landing on the uncut grass outside. There was a scary sounding *clang* – then a roar from inside as the whole shed started to shake.

"It's going to take off!" yelped Jimmy. He dashed out of the back door and ran over to the shuddering shack. Putting his hand on the door handle, he braced himself and wrenched the door open.

"All right, Jimmy?" said Grandpa.

"Hi, Grandpa," Jimmy replied, peering down the slope into the underground lab.

Grandpa looked like a crazy scientist with his wild hair and brass goggles. There was soot all over his face and oil spattered on his navy-blue overalls. In his hands he held a large silver rocket which was buzzing dangerously like it contained thousands of angry wasps. Before Jimmy could move, a huge jet of blue flame erupted from it, heading straight for him!

CHAPTER TWO
Upgrades and Add-Ons

"AAAAHHHH!" cried Jimmy as he felt the heat whoosh towards him. He quickly dived into a nearby bush.

"Whoops!" said Grandpa. "I'm glad you came over. You're just in time to see the new attachment I've built for Cabbie."

"Whoops?" muttered Jimmy, hauling himself out from the shrub and patting himself down to make sure nothing was broken. He put his hands to his face, checking that the heat blast hadn't burned his eyebrows off, and tried not to think about the fact that he'd nearly been made into a barbecued schoolboy.

Then he pulled a twig from his hair and went into the shed.

Inside, Grandpa was turning dials on the rocket and muttering to himself. Jimmy knew that look – it meant Grandpa was making calculations in his head that most people wouldn't be able to do even with a computer. All around him the gleaming white workshop was filled with hundreds of gadgets and gizmos, which clicked, whirred, steamed, puffed and fizzed away as Grandpa conducted crazy experiments and invented weird and wonderful things. And in the centre of the laboratory sat Grandpa's greatest invention of all – Cabbie.

"Hiya, Cabbie. You're looking good!" said Jimmy.

Cabbie's headlights flashed when he heard Jimmy's voice. "I know! I'm trying out a new car wax. Extra shiny," said the robot in his chirpy voice. "Watch where you're sticking that thing, Wilf. Don't scratch the paintwork!"

Grandpa bent down and started attaching the deadly weapon he had nearly fried Jimmy with to the side of Cabbie's bodywork with a welding torch. The rocket now matched another shiny missile-shaped contraption on the other side.

"It's a nitro-blaster. All those other racers will be making improvements after the last race, so I've had to work hard to upgrade your old boosters. Fire these blasters during the race and Cabbie should have the edge on any of them," said Grandpa.

"Finally, some real power!" said Cabbie. "I don't know about you, Jimmy, but I'm hungry for first place. Let's test them out!"

"Okey dokey!" said Grandpa. "Stand back!"

Jimmy ducked and held on to his eyebrows as he ran out of the way. Grandpa leaned into Cabbie's cockpit and checked that the handbrake was on, then he flicked a switch on Cabbie's dashboard and the flame shot out, making the racer lurch forward. If the handbrake hadn't been on, Cabbie would have taken off like a firework!

"Not bad, eh?" said Grandpa as he calmly reached for a fire extinguisher and sprayed it at a nearby workbench which had just caught fire. Jimmy had a suspicion it wasn't the first time he'd had to use it today. "Needs some adjustment, but it's almost there. During the race, you'll only be able to use the blasters for a short period," he added. "We need to be careful with the nitro-blasters, though. They're very delicate. If they're not treated right, they could be dangerous."

"How dangerous?" Jimmy asked.

Grandpa didn't answer, but Jimmy saw him glance guiltily up at the ceiling, where a large black burn mark was still smoking. He brushed some soot from his moustache and hurried to the other side of the lab.

Jimmy noticed how busy the workshop was looking. Experiments were taking place everywhere. Chemicals were bubbling on Bunsen burners, machines were opening and shutting parachutes, spinning tyres until they smoked, and blinking lights off and on. A strange contraption in the corner was pouring hot brown liquid into a glass beaker. Grandpa took it, peered into it, shook it around for a bit and sipped at the contents.

"Aah! Automatic tea-maker," he said, nodding at his invention. "Most important machine in this shed."

"Oi!" said Cabbie, his headlamps lighting up.

"Apart from you, Cabbie!" Jimmy laughed. "How are you? Will we be ready for the next race?"

"The Rainforest Rampage? Of course we will!" said Cabbie. "I'm like a new robot! I'm tuned up, kitted out and ready to go! My engine is in better shape, I've had a full buff and polish, and even had all my bulbs changed. Here, Wilf! Show Jimmy some of my latest modifications."

Grandpa had just sat down in a moth-eaten armchair in the corner of the lab. "Can't a man grab a quick cup of tea in peace?" he grumbled. "Hold this." He got back to his feet, passed Jimmy his beaker and climbed into Cabbie's passenger seat.

"Why does this smell of petrol?" asked Jimmy, sniffing the thick brown tea.

"It's just how I like it," shrugged Grandpa. "Now, the next race is in the jungles of South America, so I thought we should be prepared for whatever Lord Loonpipe has up his fancy sleeves."

"*Leadpipe,*" corrected Jimmy. He knew that Grandpa hated Lord Leadpipe because the billionaire had made his fortune from ideas he'd stolen from Grandpa's lab. And Jimmy knew it was part of the reason why Grandpa wanted Jimmy to win the Robot Races Championship so badly.

Grandpa carried on, his train of thought not even derailed. "The jungle is very swampy, so in case we run into some quicksand, I've installed an EFD."

"What's an EFD?" Jimmy replied.

"Glad you asked!" Grandpa grinned. "It's an Emergency Floatation Device." He reached across the dashboard and hit a button. Jimmy heard a loud hissing sound. From underneath Cabbie's bodywork a sheet of orange rubber appeared and rapidly started to fill with air. Cabbie soon had an inflatable cushion around him, like he was wearing a bright orange skirt.

"Is that our old rubber dinghy?" asked Jimmy.

"No. It *used* to be our old rubber dinghy. Now it's an EFD."

"It suits you, Cabbie!" Jimmy laughed.

"You don't think it looks like I'm wearing a dress?" asked Cabbie anxiously.

Jimmy tried to hide a grin. "No, I think you look very stylish."

Grandpa hit another button and a compartment in the bonnet opened up. "If we get into a tight spot," he said, "I've installed some grappling hooks. Just press this button and they'll shoot out, grab hold of the nearest tree branch and winch you to safety."

He pushed the button and two pronged hooks

made out of bits of scrap metal and discarded wire flew out from Cabbie's bonnet. The sharp hooks bounced off the ceiling, whistled past Jimmy's right ear and plunged straight into Cabbie's inflatable EFD.

A loud hiss filled the room.

"I'll, er, fetch the puncture repair kit," said Grandpa with a sheepish grin, getting out of Cabbie and hurrying across the workshop.

"Come and have a seat, Jimmy!" said Cabbie, his other door popping open. "There's even a little surprise inside."

Jimmy came round to the driver's seat and sat down. He saw that Grandpa had updated the dashboard. Where the old radio used to be, there were now more confusing gadgets and switches and buttons than ever, including—

"A TV!" smiled Jimmy, settling into the comfy seat. "What's on, Cabbie?"

"Just the one channel, Jimmy – Robo TV!"

Robo TV was a channel that only showed Robot Races. It had all the big competitions and got all the best interviews with racers and their robots. Jimmy switched it on and waited for it to warm up. Everything that Grandpa installed into Cabbie was re-used and recycled and the small TV had obviously been saved from a skip somewhere. Grandpa had used his electronic wizardry to turn it into a multi-functional touch-screen TV with optional voice commands. It needed a firm whack with the palm of Jimmy's hand to get going, but it was still pretty impressive. The picture finally cleared and Jimmy recognized the face of Brent Hasburger, Robo TV's smooth anchorman, as he sat behind a desk and introduced the warm-up to the next race.

"Well, I hope you brought your sunscreen, race fans, because the competition is hot, hot, hot! We're coming to you live from Manaus, Brazil, where preparations are underway for the second race of this special Robot Races championship."

"Great!" said Jimmy. "Maybe we'll get some new information on the track."

Brent Hasburger smoothed down his oily black hair and smiled at the camera. "Of course, we don't have any more information about the track—"

"Oh." Jimmy sighed.

"—as those details are being kept top secret. Jenny

Velour is at the site."

The image changed to show a reporter with a microphone. Behind her was a giant steel wall with some trees poking over the top. A big military helicopter hovered above the wall, winching down a large section of concrete track to the ground.

"Thank you, Brent. Lord Leadpipe's track builders have been in this area of the Amazon for weeks now, designing and building the new race track. Secrecy is very important, and the area has been fenced off so people are not able to see inside. Aircraft have even been banned from flying overhead, in case someone takes a photograph of the site from the air. We know little about the layout ... well, we don't know anything at all actually. Not even the racers know what will happen to them in this epic two-day race, but the experts have come up with a few suspected features."

"They're not being much help, are they?" Jimmy sighed. "They're just guessing!"

The screen now showed images of the jungle and the dangers that Jimmy might come across.

"Lord Leadpipe has been known to leave the track as a mud road for some of the way in previous competitions. The humid weather will make for a very soggy track, so off-road tyres might be a smart move. Quicksand is also a danger—"

"Told you!" said Grandpa, who had just stepped back into the shed.

"—so is the risk of mudslides on the higher land and tree falls across the roads. And that's not all. The jungle will also be full of wild animals, and our brave racers will have to be on their guard during their overnight stop-off, just in case one of these fearsome fellows decides to visit."

The screen showed jaguars, spiders and insects looking menacing, and Jimmy started to feel nervous.

"Don't worry, Jimmy!" said Cabbie. "If we can cope with Horace Pelly and that dolt of a robot of his, we can cope with a few creepy-crawly spiders!"

"No one knows what challenges Lord Leadpipe himself has planned," continued Jenny on the telly. "But we suspect that the contestants will stay overnight at this luxury campsite in the very heart of the jungle."

"Ooooh..." sighed Jimmy as the TV showed aerial pictures of a beautiful jungle clearing, with ladders leading up tall trees. Small huts had been built into the tree canopies, with rope bridges linking them. There was even a building that looked like a deluxe garage facility for all the robots to sleep in.

"That looks very posh!" said Grandpa, watching over Jimmy's shoulder. "I hope they've got tea-making facilities."

Brent Hasburger reappeared on the screen. "And now let's hear what the contenders have to say about the upcoming challenge."

A whooshing Robo TV logo flashed onto the screen, followed by the title "The Contenders".

First came Missy, the loud Australian with the monster truck. She was tinkering with Monster's oil while talking loudly to the camera: "You think I'm afraid of a few jungle creepy-crawlies? In Australia, we have spiders that can bite your arm off! As for the track, there isn't one built that I couldn't drive Monster through blindfolded."

The interviewer laughed politely.

"No, really!" said Missy. "We've been practising. It's a bit hit and miss at the moment..." The camera moved to look over Missy's backyard, where a number of crushed-looking cars sat in pieces.

Next was Kako, the Japanese princess. She sat and played a game on her 3D phone while the interviewer tried to get her attention. In the background sat Lightning, her super robobike, with five black-coated technicians polishing him and topping up his brake fluid.

"I'm sure the course will be very ... exciting." She yawned, not even raising her eyes to the camera. "I'm looking forward to the challenge. As you can see, I've worked very hard to make Lightning the best of the best." She pointed vaguely over her shoulder, where Lightning roared as he revved his engine, making the technicians jump back in fear.

"They should come and interview you, Jimmy!" said Grandpa. "You'd give 'em a good show, eh?" He took off his hat and scratched his head, sending his untidy white hair into several different directions. "Come to think of it, why haven't you been interviewed yet?"

Jimmy shrugged, and turned his attention back to the tiny TV.

Chip, the American contestant, sat in his yellow digger-like robot, Dug. "I just want a fair race, and no surprises," he said loudly. "I got tricked last time, when Horace and Zoom decided to play dirty. Well, that ain't gonna happen again, let me tell you. I'll be watching you, Horace, and you'll be watching my tail lights as I speed into first place!"

"He's a bit competitive!" said Grandpa.

"Chip? He's OK." Jimmy replied, thinking about how he'd helped the American boy in the last race. Chip hated Horace almost as much as he did!

The screen changed again to show a dry, sandy landscape. The hot sun beat down on the desert sand as a giant air-cushioned hovercraft came speeding across the square with an enormous roar. Crowds of fans whooped and clapped as the robot racer Maximus came to rest in a cloud of dust. The central cab opened and Samir, a quiet Egyptian boy in a simple T-shirt and jeans got out. He was followed by his father, Omar – a large man in racing overalls that looked a bit too small for him. The interviewer offered the microphone to Sammy, but it was immediately snatched up by his father.

"Thank you, thank you! Samir is pleased you have come to support him. Soon we travel to South

America, where we will crush the opposition! I remember when I raced in Peru almost twenty years ago..."

Sammy's father continued on with a tale of his own time in the Robot Races Championships, while Sammy stood next to him looking uncomfortable. Every time a question was asked, Omar would jump in and interrupt.

Thud! Thud! Thud!

Jimmy and Grandpa stood and stared at the door. No one had ever knocked at the door of their shed before. There was no reason to – even Jimmy hadn't known it existed until a few weeks ago. It certainly didn't look like the headquarters of a world-famous robot-racing team. Grandpa approached the door carefully.

Thud! Thud! Thud!

The two stared at each other, not sure what to do.

"Come on, get a move on!" said Cabbie. "It might be one of my fans calling for an autograph!"

Grandpa squeezed the door open, then closed it again and turned to Jimmy.

"You know I said someone should interview you?

Well, I think they've arrived!"

He let the door swing open to reveal a deafening crowd of journalists with cameras and microphones, all shouting for Jimmy!

CHAPTER THREE
Fame at Last

"Jimmy! Jimmy!"

"Jimmy Roberts, over here!"

"What's it like to be the underdog?"

"What do you think about the other contestants?"

Everyone was shouting all at once, pushing microphones at Jimmy. Flashbulbs were going off in his eyes, making them swim with pretty colours. He stood in the doorway to the shed, stunned at the gang of journalists who had suddenly appeared in his back yard.

"I … er … um…" he floundered, his mouth opening and closing like a fish, but not making a sound.

"Go on, Jimmy, they're waiting for you," said Grandpa with an encouraging nudge.

Cabbie trundled up the ramp behind them and let out an excited *parp!* on his horn. "I knew they'd finally find me! Wilf, give my bonnet a quick polish, will you – they'll want me to look my best for the photos," he said excitedly. "Come on, Jimmy, give 'em what they want!"

The sound in the garden rose to a deafening din, and Jimmy felt overwhelmed by the attention. No one had ever wanted to interview him before, and certainly not fifty people at once. He stepped back and started to close the door.

"I'm sorry, I—"

Just then he caught sight of a woman in the front row, dressed in a blue dress. She had silvery hair which was tied up in a bun, and she was waiting quietly and patiently, her microphone clutched to her chest. She smiled warmly at Jimmy as he looked at her. Jimmy recognized her at once – it was Bet Bristle, Robo TV's oldest British broadcaster. Jimmy had been watching her all his life, and she had interviewed all the great racers over the years, ever since the sport began.

"Y-you're Bet Bristle!" he stammered. The crowd went quiet.

"That's right, dear. I was wondering if I might ask you a few questions for Robo TV?" she said politely. Over her shoulder, Jimmy could see the other journalists jostling each other to try and catch their conversation.

"Me? Yes, of course."

"Excellent. Let's get you with Cabbie, shall we?" she said, her eyes darting to Grandpa, who broke out in a blush. Even though he hated Lord Leadpipe, he had always liked Bet.

Grandpa pressed a few buttons and the whole front of the garden shed rose up like a garage door, and Cabbie drove up the ramp and out to meet the crowd. He bounced his bonnet playfully and flashed his indicators at the photographers like he'd been used to fame for years.

"This is the life!" said Cabbie.

Grandpa rolled his eyes. Jimmy leaned on Cabbie's bonnet, trying to look casual as Bet started her interview.

"So how are you enjoying being a robot racer?"

she said with a smile, holding out her microphone.

"I – I love it!" Jimmy blurted out. The crowd laughed, and he felt encouraged to go on. "It's been great to compete against the other robots, and although it's all been a bit of a whirlwind, I've enjoyed every second. Also, it means I get to spend lots of time with my grandpa. He's the chief technician … actually, he's our only technician."

The crowd laughed again.

"So do you think you can win?" said Bet.

"You bet we can!" shouted Cabbie.

Jimmy silenced him with a gentle pat on the bumper. "I don't know," he said humbly. "There are so many great racers. We were lucky to take second place last time. I just hope we can do it again."

Bet smiled and glanced at the crowd of reporters. "I think he's being modest!" she said in a stage whisper. This was greeted with a chuckle and some nodding heads in the crowd. "And what have you got in store for your next race, Jimmy? It looks as though Cabbie has had a makeover."

Jimmy guided Bet over to Cabbie, showing her the new TV and the array of buttons on the dashboard.

"Grandpa's just added some new nitro-blasters which should speed us up too," he said proudly. "And the jungle can be full of dangers, so we're fully equipped with lots of gadgets to get us out of tight spots."

"How clever," said Bet, flashing a smile at Grandpa. He smiled back and went a peculiar shade of pink.

Jimmy was getting really excited. The crowd were keen to hear what he had to say, and he felt more confident by the second.

"We're ready for anything! Bring it on, Amazon! We've planned for mudslides, quicksand, wild animals, snakes—"

"*Snakes?*" Cabbie gave a moan from under his bonnet, and Jimmy darted out of the way as Cabbie's bodywork started to shake.

"What on earth...?" Bet looked confused as Cabbie's wheels whirred and span on the spot, as if he was trying to run away.

"Cabbie! *Stop!*" Grandpa jumped into the driver's seat and pulled on the robot's handbrake again.

"You never mentioned s-*snakes!*" mumbled Cabbie, his electronic voice shaking. He gave a blast of his new nitro-blasters, which sent the crowd diving to the ground, flattening themselves into the mud and grass of Jimmy's back yard to avoid the red-hot flames. His body shook again and a puff of smoke rose up from the dashboard. Cabbie lay still for a moment, and Grandpa climbed back out again. "He's overheated! He'll be all right when he calms down," he said. "Sounds like the daft old thing is afraid of snakes!"

Bet turned to face her TV camera and spoke into her microphone. "There you have it. Jimmy Roberts, the fearless underdog of the Robot Races championship, and Cabbie, his ... um ... not-so-fearless companion. This is Bet Bristle for Robo TV, in Smedingham, UK."

CHAPTER FOUR
A Message

The crowd of reporters all piled into their cars to leave. Every one of them was shouting into a mobile phone about the weird press conference they'd just been to.

"That's right," one said. "A panic attack. The robot had a panic attack!"

"He's scared of snakes, can you believe that!" said another.

"Hold the front page. There's no way the underdog's going to finish this race," yelled yet another.

Jimmy and Grandpa pushed Cabbie back into the shed and wrapped him up in a thermal blanket.

Grandpa said that this was the treatment for shock, but Jimmy wasn't so sure robots *could* be in shock.

When Cabbie finally came back online, he sounded shy and bashful.

"Cabbie, why are you afraid of snakes?" asked Jimmy.

"I don't like how they move. Slippery little things," the robot racer said. Jimmy was sure he felt the robot shudder.

"But you're a *robot*. How can a robot be afraid of anything?"

"It's my built-in personality technology. I'm programmed to be chirpy and happy ... and ophidiophobic." Grandpa and Jimmy stared at the robot blankly. "It means I'm afraid of snakes." Cabbie explained. "Keep up."

"Well, can we reprogram you?" Jimmy asked.

"Change my personality?" Cabbie said in shock. "I'm not a toaster, you know."

"He's right," Grandpa chipped in. "If we start messing around with his circuits, he could lose his current personality altogether. And we don't want to do that, do we?"

"No, definitely not," said Jimmy. "Sorry, Cabbie. I wouldn't change you for the world."

"Well, that's OK then," Cabbie said, a little calmer. "Just keep me away from any snakes and we'll be fine, Jimmy."

Just then there was another knock at the door. Grandpa got up and went to open it. "Sorry, no more interviews today!" he said as he opened the door. He stopped as soon as he saw that the person outside was not a journalist, but a short man in thick glasses and a lab coat. Jimmy noticed the familiar 'L' on his jacket. He was from Leadpipe Industries.

"Who are you?" said Grandpa.

"I'm afraid that is classified information," said the man in a thin, whiny voice. Jimmy also noticed he wore a badge which said 'Hello – My Name is Cyril'. He barged past Grandpa into the shed. "I'm here on official Robot Races business. Is this your robot?" he asked, pointing at Cabbie.

"No, it's the washing machine," snapped Grandpa, "of course he's our robot."

Cyril reached into his pocket and brought out a small computer chip held in a pair of tweezers.

"I've been ordered to make an essential upgrade, by order of Lord Leadpipe himself. Excuse me." He reached past Jimmy and clipped the computer chip to the dashboard.

"Now hang on!" said Grandpa. "No one fiddles with Cabbie except me!"

"I think you'll find the upgrade will come in useful," said Cyril, pushing his glasses up his nose. "You may need to reboot the system for it to take effect. Nice soldering on the circuit board by the way. Did you use flux-core solder wire?"

"Er, no. Lead-free," said Grandpa, sounding confused.

Cyril nodded, impressed. "Good choice," he said, and left without a word.

"What a strange chap," said Grandpa. "Go on then, let's see what Loonpipe has given us."

After a few minutes of fiddling, the TV came back on and Jimmy saw a blue screen clunk into life. On it was the familiar spinning Leadpipe Industries logo, and small icon saying 'Welcome'.

"Grandpa, what's this?" asked Jimmy.

"Search me," said Grandpa. Jimmy touched the

welcome icon and the screen filled with the face of Lord Leadpipe, to the sound of a grand fanfare.

"What does he want?" said Grandpa.

"Greetings, Racer!" said Leadpipe's disembodied head. "Thank you for accepting the RoboNet upgrade, the secure private network exclusively for robot racers."

"I didn't accept it!" said Grandpa.

"Your TV has been updated to become Cabcom, a multi-feature communications station. You can use it to talk to all the other racers in the competition, and with your technical team in the pit stop during races. Enjoy!"

The screen went back to its basic blue background, but a small envelope popped onto the screen.

"We've got a message already!" said Jimmy excitedly. He hovered his finger over the envelope and some more details appeared:

TO: CABBIE
FROM: ZOOM

"Oh, no," Jimmy sighed. He mulled over whether

to open the message for a moment or two. Then he pressed it, although as he did so, he wasn't sure if it was a good idea.

It wasn't.

Horace Pelly's smarmy face filled the screen. It was a recorded video message.

"Jimmy, hi! I thought I'd leave you a quick message to wish you good luck for the race … after all, you're going to need it in that rust bucket."

Jimmy poked his tongue out at the screen.

"My NASA guys have been improving Zoom ready for the jungle." Behind him, the screen showed a number of boffins tinkering with Zoom. "They've just fitted my new multi-point laser guidance system, the most advanced guidance technology in the world. They invented it especially for me." He produced a handheld PC which glowed with pretty lights and maps on the screen. "A satellite of my very own that tracks where I am down to the last millimetre. Look: there's me, there's you … there's a boa constrictor sliding into Cabbie's exhaust pipe…"

"WHAT?" yelled Cabbie.

On the screen, Horace started laughing. "Good

press conference by the way. Very informative. Laters, losers – I've got a race to win. See you in the jungle!" He laughed, then disappeared off the screen.

"Why, that little—" Cabbie restrained himself. Jimmy was worried now. He hoped Horace wasn't actually evil enough to release a snake near Cabbie.

Grandpa ushered him into the house and made them both some tea and jam sandwiches. Jimmy still looked worried, though.

"Don't fret about Horace Smelly, he's just a bully!" said Grandpa, ruffling Jimmy's hair affectionately. "Here, this might cheer you up." He handed Jimmy a letter to open. "I think you might be pleasantly surprised!"

Jimmy ripped it open excitedly and started reading:

Dear Mr Roberts,

Congratulations on your recent success in the Robot Races Championship. Myself and my company would like to offer some financial support in the way of sponsorship.

"Yes! Our first sponsorship deal!" said Jimmy,

punching the air and sending jammy crumbs everywhere.

"It gets better. Go on, keep reading."

That's Shallot! is Smedingham's leading supplier of fruit and vegetables and we are willing to extend a generous offer in return for advertising on the side of your wonderful robot, Cabbie.

"Hang on, it's a greengrocer's? I thought it might be ... I don't know, someone *cool*."

"They're as cool as a cucumber, Jimmy! Geddit?" Grandpa laughed. "All right, it might not be Speed-ease Trainers, but they're offering quite a deal."

Jimmy read on.

We will provide a special, top of the range, up to date model of the award-winning Carrot Vision Night Visor, as well as some more home comforts for your upcoming tour, if you agree to put our classic onion logo on your robot. We know you might not have *mushroom* in your schedule, but *lettuce* make you a sponsorship offer you can't *turnip* your nose at, and we hope someone hasn't *beet(root)* us to it!

Have a good *thyme* at the race!

Felix Crump

Jimmy groaned at the awful puns. He was embarrassed at the thought of advertising a fruit and veg company, when other robots had Luke's Lasers or Robotron Rocket Boots plastered down their sides. Then he thought back to Horace's video message, and the hive of NASA experts buzzing around Zoom. He'd never be able to afford that sort of support.

Jimmy sighed. *I suppose a bad sponsor is better than no sponsor*, he thought. *And I don't want Grandpa to think I'm ungrateful.*

"That's great news, Grandpa," he said aloud, forcing a broad smile onto his face.

"Excellent! We'll call to accept their offer in the morning," said the old man. He got up and drank the rest of his scalding hot tea, patting Jimmy on the shoulder as he walked out of the room.

Jimmy smiled, but deep down he was worried

about the race ahead. *I've got a feeling I'm going to need every modification I can get*, he thought.

Jimmy and Grandpa sat in the luxury restaurant in Lord Leadpipe's airship as it floated away from Smedingham like a gigantic airborne watermelon. They were being treated to a first-class menu from Leadpipe's personal chef. But despite the fancy surroundings, soothing music and amazing food, Jimmy had never felt so nervous. Big Al had said he was the one to beat, but he wondered if he could actually live up to the hype.

Before leaving he had watched Robo TV for hours, finding out what he could about the upgrades the other racers had put on their robots. Chip had chosen special mud-grip tyres, while Princess Kako had added Computer Assisted Stabilizing Technology (CAST) so that her bike wouldn't fall over, especially when caught in the wet mud of the jungle. Each had cost the racers a lot of money. Suddenly his Carrot Vision visor didn't seem such a great upgrade after all.

He wanted to talk to Cabbie, but he was stored at

the back of the airship with the other robots. He'd know what to say. He'd be his usual upbeat and cheery self and tell him how they were going to win fair and square, using just their wits and cunning to get to first place.

Instead, Jimmy hunched lower in his plush leather chair and picked at his meal as the aircraft angled itself south west across the Atlantic Ocean and accelerated to hyperspeed without the slightest vibration.

"Ladies and gentlemen, we are now approaching your destination. Please put on your seat belts as we prepare to land."

Jimmy woke bleary-eyed and looked around. *I must have fallen asleep*, he thought.

It had only been a couple of hours, but the super-fast airship had transported them all the way to South America. Next to Jimmy, Grandpa put down his Robot Owner's Technical Manual and gave his grandson an encouraging smile. "Time to get this show on the road, Jimmy!"

Outside the window, Jimmy could see a blanket of green across the land. Through the expanse of jungle ran a wide, vast river, snaking its way through the landscape. To his left there was a huge hilltop and perched on the top was an old ruin that looked like it had been abandoned long ago by an ancient civilization. As they descended, Jimmy could just begin to make out a shape under the trees – the Robot Races track, winding in and out of the huge trunks, and a small clearing in the jungle which he assumed would be their base camp.

"Ready to race, Jimmy?" asked Grandpa.

Jimmy smiled nervously. "Ready as I'll ever be!"

CHAPTER FIVE
Base Camp

Jimmy and Grandpa stepped down the long walkway from the airship and found themselves in the jungle clearing they had seen from the air. They walked out onto the ground, their feet sinking into the soft mud and rotting leaves underneath.

The first thing to hit Jimmy, apart from the heat and dampness, was how far away they were from anybody. He had assumed they would land in Manaus, be greeted by hordes of screaming fans and have to go overground to the start of the race, but it looked like Lord Leadpipe had other plans.

"I guess they don't trust us around the press!" said

a voice from behind them. It was Chip, in his usual baseball cap and jeans. "That's got to be the only reason to throw us this far out into the jungle!"

"I think you're right," said Jimmy. "And it's so hot and sticky out here."

"Yeah," Chip drawled. "I think I'll take a shower in my trailer."

"Trailer?" said Grandpa.

"Didn't y'all know our sponsors have been asked to provide our accommodation?" said Chip. "Here's mine now. See ya on the grid!"

Jimmy watched Chip jog off to the other side of the clearing.

"Accommodation? I can't see any accommodation," said Grandpa.

"Uh … I think he means one of those."

From the hold of the airship, an enormous robotic arm lowered a huge silver Airstream caravan into position in the clearing. The words 'Chip & Dug – Sponsored by Luke's Lasers' were written on the side. It touched down gently, the arm moved away and Chip clapped his hands. A sunshade immediately unfurled in front of the caravan, proving some much-needed shade, and steps to the main door tumbled down. Chip disappeared through the door and a moment later Jimmy could just make out the sound of rock music coming from inside.

As they stood staring, Jimmy and Grandpa watched the robotic arm place the other trailers in the clearing. Missy's was a large rough-and-ready trailer with the name of her sponsor, Robotron Rocket Boots, down one side. She hopped inside where Jimmy could see a plush sofa and games station with huge speakers.

More trailers landed, including Princess Kako's, an elegant gleaming white cube which at first looked quite small and modest. Kako pressed a button and each side expanded upwards and outwards until it became a three-storey palace. The doors slid open, and servants came out to greet her, each offering a tray of refreshments. Through the door, Jimmy saw a grand sofa facing a two-metre-high plasma wall showing Robo TV.

"Don't worry, Jimmy lad. I'm sure *That's Shallot!* have sorted out something for us," said Grandpa with a nervous smile that made his moustache wiggle.

"Um, I think this may be ours," said Jimmy, pointing

to the robotic arm extending from the zeppelin above. As it slowly descended downwards, they could see the bottom of the trailer spotted with rust. It touched down to the floor, and Jimmy gave a sigh. It was an old beige caravan with flat tyres and cracked windows. It looked a lot like the one that he and Grandpa had once stayed in for a wet seaside holiday.

On the side, in letters which were already peeling off in the humidity of the jungle, were the words *'That's Shallot!'*. Jimmy groaned with embarrassment. Grandpa ripped off a note stuck to the door:

Dear Mr Roberts,

Please accept this as a token of support. While you're preparing for victory in the jungle, we at *That's Shallot!* thought you might need some comfort and food. This trailer has air conditioning, cooling technology, and is filled with reminders of Smedingham. It may be a bit of a *squash*, but *chive* got a feeling you'll love it!

Good Luck old *bean*!
Felix Crump

Grandpa and Jimmy squeezed through the narrow door. Inside, it was so hot you could bake a potato.

"Where's the air conditioning?" said Grandpa.

Jimmy held up a tiny desk fan that sat on the table.

"And the cooling technology?"

"I think they mean the fridge," said Jimmy. He opened it to find it packed with heads of broccoli, with a label on each saying: 'Grown in Smedingham, UK'. "Yum," he said, trying to hide his disappointment.

The door of the fridge contained rows of cans of *That's Shallot!* energizing nutri-drink: '*Made from the finest ingredients – including over twelve portions of vegetables per can!*'. Jimmy slammed the door of the fridge closed, and stepped back outside.

"Hey, Jimmy! Nice digs!" shouted a familiar voice. Jimmy and Grandpa turned to see Horace with his toothy grin, standing next to his own trailer. "I could only afford a second-hand trailer too."

The trailer in question was white with some black markings on it. Jimmy had the feeling that he'd seen it somewhere before.

"Is that ... a space shuttle?" he said.

"Hmm?" Horace looked up casually. "Oh, yeah.

The NASA boys had an old one lying around, so Daddy got them to turn it into a trailer for me. It's got the basics – flat-screen TV, 3D Gaming, king-sized bed. You know, the usual."

"Ignore him, Jimmy," said Grandpa. "It doesn't matter who's got the fanciest caravan. It's all about winning the race."

"Oh, I'm going to win that as well!" said Horace. "There's no doubt about it. Look, here he comes now."

The robotic arm lowered Zoom into place beside the shuttle. Zoom's lights flashed as he said hello to Horace.

"Good trip, Zoom?" said Horace.

"Yes, thank you, Horace."

"Good. Zoom, show the nice people your new guidance system."

Zoom obediently powered up and Jimmy watched as a grid of red lasers shone from the nose of the engine.

"The multi-point laser guidance system measures the local terrain to produce a 4D map," said Zoom, sounding like a shop demonstration model. "This is fed to the hyper-accurate auto steering system, which will allow for differences in track height and width."

Horace smiled and Jimmy noticed the whole camp was watching. Sammy, the quiet Egyptian boy, had appeared by his side.

"Daddy says it's all above-board," Horace continued to boast. "He's spoken to Lord Leadpipe personally. Oh look, here's your robot, *Scabbie*."

Jimmy ignored the taunt and turned to see Cabbie being delicately placed down next to the caravan. Grandpa went to make sure Cabbie was all right after his trip.

"Zoom, scan the area for snakes. We don't want poor Scabbie to have a fright now, do we?" said Horace.

The grid of lasers expanded to fill the clearing. "No reptiles detected."

"Really?" said Horace with a grin. "We'll see about that." He disappeared into his trailer, laughing like a loon.

"Am I understanding this?" Sammy asked. "The Zoom robot will measure the distances between the trees and swamps, meaning that Horace does not have to even steer?"

"Yup," said Jimmy.

"But this is an outrage!" said Sammy. "And surely against the rules of robot racing? Why have a race with someone who does not drive?"

Jimmy was glad someone else had noticed Horace's cheating. "Horace has never really paid any attention to rules," he said with a smile. "I think that NASA put that guidance system in so that they could avoid the one faulty part in the team – Horace."

They both laughed, and Jimmy was just about to see if Sammy wanted a vegetable juice drink when they heard a shout from Sammy's trailer.

"Samir! Come here now! There is much work to be done!" Omar stuck his head out of their swanky trailer and scowled at the boys.

"But, Father, I was just speaking to Jimmy—"

"Fraternization is forbidden! Come now, we will have race tactics training!"

Sammy shrugged to Jimmy, then headed slowly back to his trailer, while Jimmy wandered over to Cabbie and Grandpa. His grandpa was now sipping at a can of veggie juice drink.

"What's it like?" asked Jimmy.

"Kind of like my world-famous cabbage stew." Grandpa said, smacking his lips together.

"Yuck!" said Jimmy, thinking how much his grandpa's cabbage stew actually tasted of old socks. Grandpa frowned. "I mean – yum!" Jimmy added quickly.

"Come on, let's get Cabbie tuned up," Grandpa said.

The clearing was soon filled with the roar of engines as each team made their final adjustments.

"How are you feeling, Cabbie?" asked Jimmy.

"I could do with a top-up of coolant, if you're offering, Jimmy."

"Me too," said Grandpa. "I'll put the kettle on."

Jimmy laughed. "Grandpa, how can you drink a hot cup of tea in this heat?"

"I'm made of strong stuff!" he joked. "And so is the tea." He went inside the caravan.

"Well, well, well, if it isn't our underdog!" Lord Leadpipe's voice boomed. The billionaire was walking around the clearing, strolling proudly around the area, shaking hands with contestants and their families.

He looked quite smart in his white linen jungle suit, his monocle glinting in the light. "I must say, your robot is quite spectacular! The others are very slick, but Cabbie here has a certain charm."

"Are you trying to say my robot is amateurish, Leadpipe?" Grandpa stood in the doorway of the caravan, a steaming cup of tea in his hand. He glared at Leadpipe, his eyes squinting.

"Wilfred," said Leadpipe, surprised. "I didn't see you there for a moment. Quite the robot, as I was saying. Have you—"

"Increased the coolant levels? Yes."

"Oh. And did you—"

"Add anti-quicksand technology? Of course."

"Right. I suppose you—"

"Adjusted tyre pressure for the soft mud track. Yes, Ludwick, I did."

An uneasy silence spread through the jungle. Even the monkeys and the parrots in the trees seemed to stop their screeching in order to watch the two old men stare each other out.

"Yes, well. Some wise upgrades. Good luck for the race." Lord Leadpipe started to stroll off towards

Samir and Maximus's camp.

"Yes, I do know a thing or two about robots," said Grandpa. "As *some people* know, I've been inventing them for years."

Lord Leadpipe stopped dead in his tracks, and turned slowly back to face Grandpa, who folded his arms and looked pointedly back. The billionaire seemed genuinely confused, his smooth, confident manner shaken for a moment.

AWOOGA! AWOOGA!

They were interrupted by a siren echoing through the forest, followed by an electronic voice.

"FIVE MINUTES TO RACE TIME. REPEAT: FIVE MINUTES TO RACE TIME."

Lord Leadpipe consulted his pocket watch and dashed off, his assistants following behind.

"Right, if everyone's finished with the small talk," said Cabbie, revving his engine excitedly, "we've got a race to win!"

CHAPTER SIX
Get Set – Go!

Cabbie screeched to a halt on the start line. As they had finished in second place in the last race, it meant that they took second place on the grid, behind Princess Kako and Lightning.

"Are you ready, Jimmy?" Cabbie asked.

"I think so," said Jimmy. "Just nervous. You?"

"Nervous? Me? No way! This is what I was built for. Can't wait!"

The Cabcom on Cabbie's dashboard fizzed and crackled. Jimmy hit it a few times with his fist until the image became clear. It was Grandpa. He was wearing a large pair of headphones over his wild white hair, and a microphone next to his mouth.

"BASE TO CABBIE! BASE TO CABBIE! ARE YOU RECEIVING? OVER."

Jimmy had to cover his ears. "Grandpa, there's no need to shout! Yes, we can hear you."

"Sorry!" said Grandpa with a grin. "I'm used to my old taxi radio. Anyway, I'll keep in touch and contact you when you need to come into the pit stop. Just remember to keep your wits about you. I'm cheering for you, lad! Good luck!"

Jimmy took a deep breath and looked around. There was Lightning in front of him and Chip – on his digger-like racer, Dug – directly behind. Horace was behind him, shouting orders to the NASA crew who were performing last-minute checks on Zoom. Next was Monster, the huge four-wheeled beast driven by Missy, who wore a scarily determined expression on her face. She revved the engine so loudly that Monster sounded like a jumbo jet.

At the very back was the huge Egyptian hovercraft-like robot, Maximus, piloted by Sammy. His father was shouting from the sidelines, but to Jimmy it sounded more like he was bossing his son around rather than encouraging him. "Remember, Samir, full throttle!" he yelled. "Take no prisoners! Failure is not an option!"

Above them all hovered the Leadpipe Industries airship, and lots of smaller safetybots and camerabots that were streaming the race live to a hundred million fans across the world. To the sides sat the audience, thousands of fans who had finally been allowed into the enormous grandstands lining the track, every one of them wide-eyed as they took in the scenes below them.

Some were staring through binoculars at the strip of red, muddy track which stretched far into the distance, trying to spot the challenges that lay ahead for the racers; others were taking photos, snapping away with their flashes blinking like fireflies; and some were chanting their favourite competitor's name and waving banners.

Jimmy noticed that a few banners even had his name on them, which made him grow in confidence. One said: 'COME ON CABBIE!' and another read: 'WE ♥ JIMMY!"

"Looks like we're starting! Better put on a show for our fans, eh, Jimmy?" said Cabbie as Jimmy pulled his battered old helmet on. The front of it was painted with the *That's Shallot!* onion logo to match the one that had been painted on Cabbie's bodywork.

The crowd hushed as the engines revved, and Lord Leadpipe stood at the start line, a microphone in his hand.

"Five!" he yelled, his voice echoing over the loudspeakers.

"Four!" This time the crowd joined in.

"Three! Two!"

The last second seemed to last for a lifetime.

"*One! Go, go, GO!*" Leadpipe shouted. The race was on!

Tyres squealed, wheels spun, and for a second everything was a blur. The robots struggled to get a grip on the road, then they suddenly lurched forwards. Jimmy was thrown back in his seat as Cabbie accelerated at a tremendous pace. He tapped the gear paddle once, twice, three times as the taxi picked up speed. Alongside him Princess Kako and Lightning were making a good start, easing away from the competition and positioning themselves for the best angle into the first corner.

Jimmy felt the ground rumbling dangerously. He checked his rear-view mirror to see Chip and Dug behind him, leading the other racers, powering forward until they were right on Cabbie's tail. The size of the digger-like robot was terrifying, the deep noise from the engine drowning out the high-pitched revs coming from underneath Cabbie's bonnet. Chip was having no trouble steering Dug's caterpillar track wheels on the red clay roads, but Cabbie's tyres were already slipping and sliding.

"Take it a little bit slower," said Grandpa over the Cabcom. "We don't want to risk a crash."

Jimmy eased off the gas slightly and took the bend cautiously, allowing Chip room to pull alongside. Behind them, Monster's giant wheels were also tearing up the terrain. Missy dived to the right of Jimmy, and for a moment he was boxed in between two giant robot racers. The noise of their engines was deafening and the ground was shaking so much they could easily have been in the middle of an earthquake. Jimmy could feel the vibrations from the steering wheel travelling up through his arms and jangling his bones so hard that it made his teeth chatter. He was almost relieved when the two heavy vehicles swept past him. But it did mean that Jimmy and Cabbie were down into fourth place.

"See ya!" shouted Missy as she cruised past the rest of them and into the lead. As Monster increased in speed, her giant tyres kicked up mud and sprayed it all over the other robots.

"Yuck!" said Jimmy. "Cabbie, I'm turning on the windscreen wipers." He flicked on the wipers and the screen cleared.

Cabbie and Maximus were neck and neck now, and Jimmy glanced across to see Sammy practically blinded by the mud splattered over his windscreen. He was panicking in his cab, and over the Cabcom Jimmy could hear Samir's father barking orders: "ENGAGE VISION CLEANSER! FASTER, CHILD!"

Jimmy flicked on the Cabcom screen and pressed on a button that said SAMIR AND MAXIMUS. The Cabcom immediately showed Sammy in the driving seat, desperately searching for a button. "You OK, Sammy?" Jimmy asked.

"Yes – aha, got it!" Sammy said, flicking a switch. "Oops—" he added as a burst of blue energy fired

Maximus high into the air, bunny-hopping down the track before spinning 360° and coming to a stop.

"Look out!" Cabbie yelled. Jimmy had been so busy watching Sammy he'd forgotten to pay attention to his own driving. He had to swerve wildly to avoid a thick curtain of vines hanging down from the tree canopy. He veered to the other side of the track and managed to get skid past them without slowing down, but Zoom wasn't so lucky. Horace must have seen the vines too late and the sports car hit them full on, sending Zoom spinning out of control.

"Yikes!" said Jimmy. "That'll slow them down for a bit."

It took all of his concentration to keep Cabbie on the road for the next twenty miles. The track was proving to be a bigger challenge than his fellow racers, with huge holes in the dirt road jarring Jimmy's spine, and hidden tree stumps and vines to avoid. Jimmy was glad he could rely on Cabbie's navigation to help him avoid an accident.

"We haven't seen any of the others for ages," Jimmy said after a while. "I'm beginning to think we'll never catch Dug, Monster or Lightning."

But just then they passed a flash of silver and reddish-brown on the roadside. Princess Kako was drenched in mud, her bright leathers covered in gloopy Amazonian clay. As Cabbie whizzed on by, Jimmy could see a furious Kako using all her strength to pull a sharp stake of wood from Lightning's back tyre. She had a serious puncture.

"She won't like that," said Jimmy. "I wonder if she'll be able to fix it."

"She'll be fine," replied Cabbie. "Once she gets that chunk of tree out of Lightning he'll activate his automatic tyre repair system. They'll be back on our tail in no time if we don't hurry."

"Let's get a move on, then!" said Jimmy.

Over the next few miles the road got smoother and they slowly began to close the gap on the racers in front. Soon Jimmy could see the Dug in the distance, thundering along the course and driving between the giant trees that lined the track.

"Right, it's time to unleash our special weapon," said Grandpa over the com system. "Jimmy, the track widens out in a few hundred metres. It might be a good opportunity to overtake on Chip's right."

"What? We'll never be able to get past before the road narrows again." Jimmy exclaimed.

"That's where these come in," said Cabbie, and a small button lit up on the dashboard, flashing blue.

Jimmy recognized it. The nitro-blasters. He gulped.

"Come on, Jimmy. You worry too much!" said Cabbie.

"All right," Jimmy answered, bracing himself. "Let's see what you can do."

"Yes! Hold onto your helmet, Jimmy!" the robot replied.

Jimmy positioned Cabbie to the right of the track and reached out to the flashing blue button. He held on tight, and pressed it.

Ssssssccccccccccccchhhhhhhhhhhhhhhuuu!

The next thing Jimmy knew, his head was pressed against his racing seat like it was superglued to it, and Cabbie was hurtling along the track faster than a fighter jet!

CHAPTER SEVEN
Sonic Boom

"Yeeee-haaaa!" shouted Cabbie as they were propelled forward by the nitro-blaster.

"Aaaaaaagh!" screamed Jimmy, his hands gripping the steering wheel so tight that he left marks where his fingernails had dug in.

Cabbie zoomed ahead, a ribbon of blue flame licking out of the boosters mounted on each side of him. The camerabots had to spin around overhead to keep up with them, and they were still accelerating.

"This ... is ... amazing!" Jimmy tried to say, but the G-force was making the skin on his face wobble about so much that it was hard to speak.

"We've still got the best bit to come – the sonic boom!" said Cabbie, who was clearly loving every second.

"Sonic what?" Jimmy gasped out.

"Never mind. Ready? Three … Two … One…"

BOOM!

The humid forest air shook as Cabbie broke the sound barrier. Beautiful birds of paradise scattered and monkeys screeched behind them as they raced through the forest and drew alongside Dug. But they were running out of space. The track was getting narrower and narrower again, and they could see they were approaching a sharp left turn.

"We're not going to make it!" yelled Cabbie. "There's no way we can turn the corner at this speed!"

"We'll make it!" said Jimmy over the loud engine. "Do you trust me?"

"What? Why?"

"I've got a plan. Do you trust me?"

"Yes!"

"Then turn off the left nitro-blaster in three … two … one … *NOW, CABBIE!*"

Cabbie shut down the rocket on his left side, and

just when it looked like they were going to crash, they whipped into a tight arc. The right blaster slingshot them round the bend like they were on a ride at a theme park, missing Dug's front bumper by millimetres.

Then *bam!* Jimmy hit the blue button again and the right nitro-blaster shut down, leaving Cabbie perfectly lined up on the next straight.

"Wow!" said Jimmy, a little dazed.

Grandpa appeared on the Cabcom screen, a huge smile hanging under his white moustache. "Jimmy, you did it! You did it, my boy." Jimmy could see him dancing a little jig. "You wouldn't believe what the commentators are saying about you. They reckon that's the best move they've seen in years."

Jimmy's chest swelled with pride, but he knew that he still had lots to do.

"How are you holding up, Cabbie," he asked his robot racer.

"Ha!" laughed Cabbie. "Never been better. I was amazing. And Jimmy, you weren't too bad either. That was *brilliant!*"

As he looked down the long, straight track in

front of them, Jimmy eased his grip on the steering wheel a little. Far ahead, he could see Monster trundling along, kicking up dirt and dust. His next job was to overtake Missy, but he had just noticed something else...

"Cabbie—"

"That's how we roll, Jimmy baby! Robot-racer style!"

"Cabbie, look!"

"If I had hands, I'd give you a high-five!"

"Cabbie, look out!" Jimmy wrenched the wheel to the right as they drove straight towards another thick section of vines. Cabbie's tyres screeched as they avoided the vines before Jimmy flicked the wheel back to keep them safely on the road.

"That was close," Jimmy said.

"Oops," said Cabbie, his electronic voice sounding embarrassed. "I guess I got carried away and stopped paying attention for a second there."

Jimmy smiled. "That's OK. It *was* pretty awesome."

Up ahead, the brake lights on Missy's truck told him she was slowing down to a crawl, and when they got closer they found out why. The track had narrowed so that Monster's massive wheels only just fitted on the road. Either side of the track was a swamp, with overhanging trees making it seem dark and creepy. With no room to pass on either side of the monster truck, Jimmy had no choice but to slow down to a crawl behind Missy, and wait for a chance to overtake her.

"Come on, come on!" said Cabbie. "Can't we honk at her? It always worked when I was a regular taxi."

"Did it?"

"Well, no, but it made me feel better. What about chancing it in the swamp? It can't be that deep. Don't forget, we've got the rubber dinghy. I mean, the EFD."

Jimmy glanced at the murky water on either side of the track. He was just about to agree and drive into the swamp when he saw a ripple on the surface and lots of tiny flashes of white light.

"Cabbie, can we get the internet on the Cabcom?" Jimmy asked.

"This is no time to check your email," said Cabbie. But he fired up the Cabcom so it came up with the official Robot Races website.

"Search 'wildlife'," Jimmy said, and the screen

displayed some options of pages to look at. It showed the different places around the world that Robot Races took place. "Choose 'Amazon swamps'," he said. A page of information popped up. "Activate speech."

The Cabcom burst into life. A soft woman's voice filled the cab, reading the information that was displayed on the screen, leaving Jimmy to steer.

"*The swamps of the Amazon jungle are filled with dangerous animals. The most deadly are probably the great electric eels. The swamps are their natural habitat, and they feed off tiny fishes and insects, but if disturbed they can emit powerful charges of electricity.*"

"Hmm, so that's what those flashes are," said Jimmy. "They're from giant electric eels! Hundreds of them, by the look of it. Even if we managed to float across there, one false move and the eels would attack."

The American voice on the Cabcom continued. "*The eels hunt in packs. Combined, they could generate enough electrical charge to power a city.*"

"In other words," said Jimmy, "they'd fry your motherboard."

Cabbie was unusually quiet for a moment. "Yikes," he said eventually.

"But you're right." Jimmy said, staring at Monster's bumper. "We can't just sit here. What else have you got?"

Cabbie ran though his upgrades and add-ons, but there didn't seem to be anything that would help. "I'll activate the headlights," he said. "These overhanging trees make it so dark in here."

"The trees! That's it! We can overtake easily!" said Jimmy with a new energy in his voice. "We can use the grappling hooks to grab hold of the trees above!"

"Of course!" said Cabbie, catching on to the idea. "I can winch us in so fast that we'll sail through the air and land on the other side of Missy and Monster!"

Jimmy imagined the scene. "Leapfrogging a monster truck could work, but it will be dangerous."

"I like it," Cabbie said, sounding excited. "We'd be jumping – actually *jumping* – into first place!" Cabbie sounded excited. "It's a genius idea, Jimmy. Let's do it!"

CHAPTER EIGHT
A Risky Move

Jimmy knew what he had to do. He tightened his seat belt and closed his eyes. "Let's go."

"Wicked!" said Cabbie. "Deploying grappling hooks." A compartment on the bonnet slid open and the hooks raised up like missiles getting ready to launch. "Identifying target."

Cabbie's sensors quickly mapped the area and found the perfect tree to target – a large strong one with a branch that extended out over the track.

"Go for it, Cabbie!" said Jimmy. "*FIRE!*"

The hook fired, sending more birds and wildlife scattering. It bounced off the branch and Cabbie quickly reeled it in. "Drat! I'll adjust the elevation," he said.

Just then, Jimmy heard a sound from behind him. He looked to see Dug on the track a few hundred metres behind him. If they waited much longer every one of the racers would be tucked up behind Cabbie's boot.

"Cabbie, we need to go, now!" he said.

"OK! Ready ... aim ... *fire!*"

Jimmy pressed the button. The hook flew up again, sailing over the monster-truck racer and biting deep into a thick, broad branch.

"Here we go!" Cabbie shouted as he activated the powerful winch.

"Woah!" shouted Jimmy, surprised at how quickly they left the ground. They swung through the air like Tarzan, gaining speed, the branch creaking under their weight. Just when they reached the halfway point, Jimmy looked down at the top of Monster and the swamp on either side of her, which was flashing with angry electric eels.

"Preparing to cut cable," said Cabbie.

Jimmy panicked. "What? You never said anything

about cutting anything!"

"It's the only way, Jimmy. Trust me!"

Jimmy held onto the steering wheel for dear life as a blade on the winch cut through the tough steel coil as easily as a knife slicing through soft cheese. For a moment, Cabbie and Jimmy hung in mid-air above the track and the swamp, nothing supporting them except the humid air of the jungle. Jimmy felt as if they were floating like Lord Leadpipe's airship, and for a second everything was peaceful and quiet. Until, that is, gravity took hold and they began to drop. Cabbie was still moving forward, the swing of the rope having done its job. Jimmy yelled out loud as they sailed through the air with all the grace and beauty of a flying brick.

"Waaaaagh!"

WHOMP! They landed with a hard bump on the track, about ten metres ahead of a confused-looking Missy.

"Woooo-hooooo!" cheered Cabbie. "Bull's-eye!"

Jimmy had to do some nifty steering so they didn't career into the swamp. Once he'd got Cabbie under control, he pressed the accelerator hard and they sped off down the track. They raced past the swamp and out into the jungle, where the track spread out a little and they were really able to pick up the speed.

"Don't – you – *ever* do that again!" shouted Jimmy.

"Sorry, I should have warned you about cutting that cable. But look—" Cabbie turned on the official Robot Races tracking system, a map of the course with small coloured dots showing the positions of the competitors. "We're in first place!"

Jimmy looked, and sure enough, there was their small blue dot in front, with Missy behind and Dug and Lightning still somewhere in the swamp. Sammy and Kako were close behind them. Strangely, Jimmy couldn't see Horace and Zoom on the map at all.

"OK," said Jimmy. "You were lucky."

"I was a *genius*."

"Whatever!" Jimmy laughed.

Grandpa's face appeared on the Cabcom. "You're in first place!" he announced.

"We know!" said Jimmy and Cabbie together.

"Good show, lads! The commentators are calling it the maddest – move in the history of Robot Races!" Jimmy was strangely proud of that. "You obviously don't need my help, which is just as well. The airship is coming to take the parents and technicians to the base camp for the night. You'll be there in no time, and we can repair and refuel there."

"And eat! I could eat a horse!" said Jimmy.

Grandpa laughed. "I don't know about a horse but I've got a sack of cabbages from *That's Shallot!* we can tuck into."

Yuck! thought Jimmy.

In the background of the picture, Jimmy could see the other teams talking to their racers on headsets. Mr Pelly was talking in a quiet voice, while Omar Bahur was barking instructions so loudly in Arabic that Jimmy could hear him clearly, even if he couldn't understand what he was saying. Grandpa leaned into the camera, his wrinkly face and white hair filling the screen.

"Between you and me, I reckon old Mr Pelly is up to something. As well as that fancy laser navigation system Zoom's got, he's also been feeding Horace information all day, looking at old maps and charts. Some of them are ancient. They must be from when the first explorers landed here."

"Hmm, that is strange," said Jimmy, remembering that Zoom had been missing from the tracking system map earlier. "Keep an eye on him, will you, Grandpa? See you at the camp."

"Will do. Over and out!"

Jimmy finally relaxed and sped up, confident that no one was going to catch them for the rest of the day. Everyone had got stuck behind Missy in the swamp, and Cabbie was now in the lead by miles. He sat back, put Cabbie into cruise control for a while and whistled a happy tune.

WOOOOOOSH!

Jimmy grabbed the wheel and continued steering as something whizzed past them. He looked over to see a sleek black sports car fly past him at an alarming speed. Jimmy couldn't believe his eyes, but it was true.

They had just been overtaken by Horace and Zoom!

CHAPTER NINE
A Race Between Rivals

"Impossible!" said Cabbie, after his robot recognition software had confirmed it was them. "They came out of nowhere!"

"Cabbie, did we go the right way? How did they get ahead of us?"

"I don't know. I'm the best navigator there is, and I can't work out how they did it!"

Jimmy sped up again, trying to catch Zoom at the next bend. There was no time to sit back and relax any more. The race had just got interesting again!

"They must have found a hidden short cut!"

Jimmy shook his head, refusing to believe it.

The rumour was that track builders put a hidden short cut in every race. If you found it, you could skip a whole section, which could mean the difference between first place and last. But in the entire time that Jimmy had been watching the races, no racer had ever found one. No one really knew whether Lord Leadpipe put them in when he designed the tracks, or if they were just a robot races myth.

"Maybe Horace found a short cut using his fancy laser guidance system." Jimmy thumped the steering wheel in frustration.

"Ow!" said Cabbie.

"Sorry." Jimmy patted Cabbie's dashboard.

They took the bend and the track widened. Cabbie started to overtake, but Zoom matched his speed. Jimmy glanced over to see Horace in the driver's seat, smiling and waving sarcastically. He reached out a finger and pressed something on his dashboard.

"Waaah!" yelled Cabbie, lurching to the side. Jimmy looked out of the window to see what had happened. Flame-throwers had suddenly appeared from the middle of Zoom's wheels, sending huge yellow jets of fire towards Cabbie! The flames reached out and nearly touched his tyres. Jimmy could feel the heat from the driving seat.

"HOTHOTHOTHOT!" shouted Cabbie.

"Let's drop back!" ordered Jimmy. "The tree canopy's so thick around here that the race organizers won't have seen Horace cheating."

No, I can take it," Cabbie said. "This is our race. We can't let him bully us."

Jimmy didn't object any more, but he could smell the unmistakable stench of burning rubber from Cabbie's wheels as the tyres heated up. He kept Cabbie to the far side of the track and away from the flames, but he didn't have much room before he would be pushed off the edge. If the flames got any closer, the tyres could set alight and explode.

The Cabcom bleeped and the screen was filled with Horace Pelly's tanned face.

"Afternoon, losers!" he smiled.

"Turn off the flame-throwers, Horace!" Jimmy demanded.

"Oh, is that what that button does?" Horace laughed. "Give up, then," he ordered.

"No chance!" shouted Jimmy. "I don't take orders

from cheats like you, Pelly!"

Horace's face dropped into a scowl. "My laser guidance system is perfectly within the rules, and better than your Scabby Cabbie's navigation system. I'm surprised *That's Shallot!* didn't buy you a new one. I hear you're helping their business tremendously at the moment – people just look at you and say, 'What a lemon!'"

Horace laughed like a hyena and Jimmy hit the Cabcom screen to make him disappear. The track led them towards a clearing in the forest and Jimmy was determined he was going to get there first. But when Horace saw that Jimmy wasn't going to drop back, he redirected all power to Zoom's engines. The flame-throwers went out, and the sleek black robot powered forward towards the clearing.

They were still neck and neck as Jimmy saw the clearing ahead. Rising up in the centre of the open space was a gigantic stone statue with carvings on its sides. It looked like the totem poles that he had read about at school, and he guessed it must have been put there by an ancient civilization which had once lived in the jungle. Totem poles were meant to scare off evil spirits, but at that moment Jimmy just wished this one could get rid of Horace Pelly.

They roared into the open and Jimmy was surprised when Zoom veered to one side, choosing not to take the most direct line across the clearing.

"This is our chance, Jimmy!" said Cabbie

"Are you sure? Why isn't Zoom going that way?" Jimmy asked.

"We don't have time to argue! Go for it!"

Jimmy dropped back a few metres and overtook Zoom on the other side, edging around him. He could have sworn he saw Horace smirk. Then Horace grabbed Zoom's controls, gripped the steering wheel and threw his robot racer to the right. Zoom lurched right, the strong black metal exterior crunching as it hit Cabbie.

"Ow!" said Cabbie as he lurched to one side. "He rammed us!" Just as he tried to recover, Zoom hit them once more, sending them careering towards the ancient stone monument.

"Brace for impact!" said Cabbie. Jimmy tensed, grabbing the seat, waiting for the crash as they hit the old totem pole.

But the crash never came. Instead, Jimmy felt the ground in front of the monument give way. He saw the trees around him rush upwards and his stomach jumped like he was in a fast-dropping elevator.

"Woah!" Cabbie yelled as his safety airbags exploded open and they hit the ground with a jolt. They had fallen right into a trap!

CHAPTER TEN
Caught in a Trap

"Jimmy? Jimmy? Are you OK?" Jimmy heard Cabbie say. It was pitch-black, and he couldn't see his hand in front of his face. "Jimmy!" Cabbie yelled more urgently.

"Yeah, I'm OK," gasped Jimmy finally.

The fall had knocked the breath out of him, and he struggled to fill his lungs. He sat still for a few more moments, checking himself over. He had bashed his head against Cabbie's door and could feel a small bump developing. His ears were ringing slightly, but Jimmy knew that it could have been much worse. The airbag and seat belt had saved him from a much nastier injury, making sure that he hadn't cracked his head on the steering wheel, or gone through the windscreen. He had bitten into his lip in the crash, and his mouth now tasted hot with blood. Otherwise he was all right, just a bit shaken up.

"Are you OK, Cabbie?" Jimmy asked as he opened Cabbie's door and stepped out shakily. He stretched, making sure all of his body parts worked, coughing out the dust which was settling around him.

"Me? I'm fine. My fenders are damaged and the only working nitro-blaster fell off when we fell. Other than that, I'm right as rain.Good job your grandpa doesn't skimp on safety devices."said Cabbie.

"I know," replied Jimmy. "That was a close call."

"Are you sure you're OK? That was still quite a fall for a human to take."

"Yeah, I'll be fine. Thanks for looking after me, Cabbie," Jimmy patted his racer's bonnet.

"No problem, partner," the robot replied. "All part of the service."

Jimmy looked up, to where sunlight poured in through a hole in the roof high above him. A shadow appeared, and for a brief moment Jimmy thought it might be a safetybot. His heart sank. If he and Cabbie had to be rescued, they'd be out of the race!

Jimmy was almost relieved when he heard Horace's smarmy voice.

"Whoopsy! Did you have a little fall?" said Horace. "You really should be more careful."

"Get us out of here, Horace!" Jimmy demanded.

"Tut-tut! You didn't say the magic word. Never mind, I'm not going to help you anyway." Horace walked around the edge of the hole like a proud peacock. "It was Daddy who found these secret chambers. He had been studying old explorers' maps from hundreds of years ago, and came across an ancient temple buried below the stone monument. It even had a warning – 'Danger! Weak Ground'. Even the track builders hadn't found it, so it'll be ages before the safetybots come to get you out."

Jimmy balled his hands into fists, feeling ready to burst. Horace had been planning this all along.

"You won't get away with this, Horace! Get me out now!"

Horace Pelly laughed, and it echoed all the way down to Jimmy. "Sorry, Jimmy. I don't take orders from *losers*. Bye bye now!"

He strolled away from the edge of the hole, and Jimmy heard him laughing as he drove away in Zoom.

"What are we going to do, Cabbie?"

"The Cabcom was damaged in the fall." Cabbie sighed. "I'll keep trying to fix it, but I think we might just have to wait for rescue."

Jimmy walked over to a pillar and placed his hand on it. It was ridged and bumpy, and Jimmy used what little light there was to see that it was covered in painstakingly carved ancient symbols. So were the walls and the dusty floor.

"Dark, isn't it?" said Cabbie. "I'd make some light, but my headlights cracked in the fall."

"*Ffzzzssshhh* ... Jimmy, Cabbie, are you receiving me? Over." Grandpa's voice was coming from the dashboard. Jimmy dashed back into the driving seat and looked at the Cabcom, which fizzled and crackled.

"Grandpa, I can hear you! Can you get help?" Jimmy could see the old man's face on the screen, but there was no reply. Until—

"Jimmy? Cabbie?" said Grandpa's worried voice. He frowned at the screen and appeared to hit the camera he was staring into. "It's no good, I've lost them again!" they heard him say.

"He can't hear us. Cabbie, can you contact him another way?"

"Sorry, Jimmy, this is the best I can do." Cabbie gave a deep sigh that rattled his bumper.

"*Pelly!*" shouted Grandpa on the screen, turning to face Horace's dad. "What has your boy done to my grandson? They were neck and neck, and now Jimmy has disappeared!"

"What on earth are you accusing me of?" asked Mr Pelly. Grandpa stood up and threw down his headset, but was shouting so much that Jimmy could still hear him. Another voice joined in, the familiar sound of Joshua Johnson, the Robot Co-ordinator.

"Gentlemen, sit down! Fighting won't solve anything!"

"We'll see about that!" There was a scuffle off-screen, and the picture flickered and faded, just as it looked like Grandpa was going to get very angry indeed.

"They sound like they're having fun," said Jimmy with a sigh. He tried hard to think of the best thing to do, struggling not to think about the fact that they could be trapped in this dark, cold tomb for ever. It would have been very easy to panic and curl up into a whimpering little ball, but there was one thing worse that being stuck: Horace Pelly getting his own way.

"This is *our* race," he said.

"Pardon?" Cabbie replied.

"This is *our* race," Jimmy repeated, with more confidence. "We were winning. And no one is going to take it away from us, especially not *him*."

With a steady look in his eye, he climbed onto the roof of Cabbie, and jumped up and down, attempting to make the leap to the ground above them. It was useless – far too high to jump. He took a deep breath and thought hard.

"Cabbie, do we still have a second grappling hook?"

"Yes."

"Excellent. Shoot for the edge of the hole above. You can winch us out and then we can contact Grandpa."

"Great plan, Jimmy!"

Cabbie engaged the grappling hook and it rose

out of his bonnet. He fired, but the first few shots landed wide of the mark, hitting the temple wall uselessly. On the fourth attempt, the home-made hook flew out towards the sky. When they reeled it in slowly, they found the sharp spikes could not get a grip and just brought soil down on top of them from the edge of the hole as it crumbled away some more. The hook fell to the floor with a depressing clang.

"It's no good," said Jimmy. He sat down on the floor, resting against Cabbie's side. He was angry for a moment with Grandpa. He was supposed to be the robotic genius with a plan for everything. Where was their upgrade for this situation? He hit his head back against the door in frustration, bashing the ridiculous cartoon onion with the words 'That's Shallot! proudly sponsors Jimmy and Cabbie' underneath. Why had they been so stupid to accept sponsorship from them? What could a fruit and veg shop do that could help them in the race?

Suddenly Jimmy was hit by an idea. It was so obvious that he could have kicked himself. He shot up with a grin.

"Carrots!" he yelled.

"What?" Cabbie asked.

"We've been so silly! We've got the night-time vision upgrade from our sponsors. Cabbie, engage Carrot Vision!"

Jimmy quickly picked up the nitro-blaster that lay on the ground next to Cabbie, and laid it carefully behind his seat. He remembered how delicate Grandpa had said it could be – and he certainly remembered the large burn mark on the ceiling of the shed! He wanted to keep hold of the blaster, just in case Grandpa could fix it back on later. Then he climbed into the driving seat and Cabbie turned the Carrot Vision on. A visor rose up from the bonnet, covering the windscreen. With it there, the whole chamber seemed to be bathed in a green glow, and suddenly they could see everything.

"Wow! Carrots really *can* make you see in the dark!" said Cabbie.

Now they had the visor they could see how big the chamber was. The walls and floor were covered in carvings. Some of the marks were in an ancient language that even Cabbie, with his language-translator chip, couldn't understand. Some were pretty designs, but others were larger and scarier: a mythical beast that was half-man, half-panther; a ferocious winged ape with teeth and claws the size of Jimmy's head; and a fish with razor-sharp fins, leaping out of the water, its eyes glinting in the green light.

"Jimmy?" said Cabbie. "What are they?"

"Gods, I suppose," he guessed. He had once watched a documentary on this sort of thing with Grandpa. "The people here used to worship them, probably bring them sacrifices. Why are you shaking?" Cabbie's engine was shuddering so hard that the broken fender was performing a tap dance on the ground outside. Jimmy felt like he was sitting on a washing machine on the spin cycle.

"Because I don't like the look of that one!"

Jimmy turned to see the biggest carving of them all, completely filling an entire wall. It was an enormous cobra, easily five metres in height, with little images of people running away from it at the bottom of the wall. Around the huge figure were dozens of smaller writhing snake carvings.

"Do you think he thinks we're one of his sacrifices?" said Cabbie with a gulp.

Jimmy didn't like the look of it either, but tried to keep calm. He searched the chamber until he found something. "Look down there!" he said suddenly.

Cabbie let out a burst of smoke from his exhaust pipe. "What? Where? Is it the Snake God? I don't see anything!" he panicked.

"Exactly! The chamber just goes on and on. If we drive down there we might just find an exit."

"Anything to get us out of here!" Cabbie said, sounding much more like his old self again.

Jimmy slammed his door shut, Cabbie started his engine and they slowly drove forwards into the dark.

They edged along the chamber, wary of any weak floors or ceilings. If they had managed to fall through a ceiling in the clearing, then the rest of the chamber could fall in at any moment. Cabbie was shaking a little less now, happy to be away from the image of the Snake God, and talking quickly.

"It's just the way they move, you know? I don't trust them, the horrible slithery things. Silly, really. And I don't like the way they poke their tongues out like that. It's just rude, that's what it is."

"I'm sure we'll be safer down here," said Jimmy.

"Sorry I got you into this," said Cabbie. "I shouldn't have told you to cut across that clearing. We would have been all right if we had kept to the path like you said. Now we're stuck."

"Don't be silly. We're a team, and we stick together. Horace led us to a trap, and he barged us into it. No one is to blame except him."

"OK!" said Cabbie, sounding even more like his old chirpy, cheery self. "Let's concentrate on getting out of here!"

But they hadn't gone more than a few metres when they heard a huge crash and an explosion behind them.

"What the...?" Jimmy exclaimed as the ground shook behind him. He looked around to see thousands of tons of stone and dirt falling from the roof as the ruins seemed to crumble around him. A cloud of dust swept towards him and rocks the size of cricket balls hurtled towards Cabbie's windows. "Watch out!" yelled Jimmy. "The roof's falling in!"

CHAPTER ELEVEN
Deeper Underground

"Are you all right?" Jimmy said when the noise of the explosion had stopped.

"Well, I'm going to need a new paint job, if that's what you mean." Cabbie joked. "And it's going to take your grandpa hours to get out all these cracks on my glasswork."

"I'll take that as a yes," said Jimmy, smiling at Cabbie's reply. "It sounded like the rockfall came from that chamber we just left. Let's go and check it out."

Cabbie did a quick handbrake turn so he was facing the other way and Jimmy poked his head out of the door, peering into the darkness. He couldn't make out what had happened, so sat back down and looked through the Carrot Vision visor.

"Cabbie, can you zoom in on that rockfall? I can't see that far."

"Sure thing! Zooming to seventy-five per cent."

The picture on the visor became larger, and Jimmy was able to understand what he was looking at. At the end of the chamber, in a cloud of dust and broken rocks, was a large hovercraft covered in soil and debris from the fall. It had fallen down in almost the exact same spot as Cabbie had earlier and it had brought down another large chunk of the jungle floor with it.

"It's Maximus!" said Jimmy. "Sammy must be in there. Let's go and help."

Cabbie rushed to the hoverbot. Sammy climbed out of his cockpit, shaken and scared.

"Jimmy? Where am I?" he said, looking dazed and confused.

"An old temple, we think. I'll explain later. Are you hurt?" He shook his head. "And Maximus?"

Maximus said something in Arabic, and Sammy translated. "His spare fuel tank has cracked, but there is no damage to the rest of him. Thankfully, the hovercraft's air cushions softened our fall. I was crossing the clearing when my father ordered me to go close to the stone monument to save time. It looked dangerous, but—"

He was interrupted by the Cabcom blaring from Maximus's cockpit, where Omar was shouting at the top of his voice, "Samir! Answer me immediately!"

The Cabcom hissed and went blank as it lost its signal. Sammy actually looked relieved. Then the walls shuddered again, and another bucketful of soil landed on top of Maximus.

"We've got to get out of here," said Jimmy.

"Yes. It is – how do you say the word? Creepy," said Sammy.

Jimmy laughed. "It's also falling down. There might be an escape route down this way."

The hole crumbled some more and another large chunk of rock fell down. It just missed Cabbie and Maximus, then rolled across the floor and struck one of the carved pillars that supported the ceiling. The pillar cracked, a small line appearing in the carvings that wound their way up to the roof.

"Uh-oh," said Cabbie.

"Let's go!" said Jimmy. "Move, move, move!"

They both hopped back into their driving seats. The motors on the robots roared as they tried to make a quick getaway. The pillar cracked and crumbled, and then with a great crash it fell to the floor, leaving the roof unsupported.

"Full throttle, Cabbie!" yelled Jimmy.

"You don't have to tell me twice!"

Cabbie and Maximus zipped along the chamber, away from the crumbling hole, and not a moment too soon. The roof and supporting walls fell in on each other with a loud crash, sending stone and dust flying. As they sped along trying to outrun the cloud of dust and rubble that chased them along the chamber, Jimmy spotted a section of wall ahead that had a gap in it. He realized it must be a corridor and at the last second he steered into it, Maximus following just metres behind. The corridor was small, and Maximus was so large that he only just fitted into it. The two racers sped along it as fast as they could, as the ceiling fell down behind them in a cloud of rock and rubble.

They slowed down, safe for the moment.

"There goes the rest of the roof," said Jimmy. "I just

hope this corridor leads to an exit, or we're trapped!"

The roof and wall of the corridor seemed more stable than the main chamber and unlikely to cave in, so they slowed down a little more, Maximus following behind. Jimmy's Cabcom lit up, and Sammy's voice came from the speakers.

"It is good thing we can use the Cabcom shortwave radio to talk to each other, yes?" he said. "Where we go now?" Jimmy thought that Sammy sounded quite perky, even happy. He might have said that he was enjoying this, if their lives hadn't been at stake.

"I haven't a clue. We'll just have to see where this takes us."

They continued along the dark passage for a while.

"How are you feeling, Cabbie?"

"Awful," moaned the robot. "My sensors keep picking up snakes in the area."

"Don't be silly. We must be about a hundred metres underground."

"My sensors don't lie, Jimmy. There's a horrible hissing sound coming from somewhere nearby."

"It's impossible. This place hasn't been used in thousands of years! Just take it easy."

Cabbie seemed to calm down a little. "You're right. I'm being daft. There's no way that there would be – *EEK!*"

Cabbie slammed on his brakes and a screech of rubber filled the corridor. Maximus ground to a halt behind him, reversing his thrusters so he didn't crash into Cabbie.

Jimmy peered ahead in the green-lit gloom and saw the reason for Cabbie's sudden manoeuvre. The floor dropped in front of them, leaving no way past. It left a pit in the floor, filled with hundreds of thin, wriggling, slithery, slimy—

"*SNAKES!*" wailed Cabbie.

They were vipers of all different colours – green tree snakes, yellow coiled vipers, orange ones, striped ones and speckled ones – all moving over each other and hissing hungrily.

"Cabbie, calm down!" Jimmy said, not feeling too calm himself.

It was no good. Just like at the press conference, the robot started to shudder and twitch, his bonnet starting to steam as he overheated.

"Get them away!" he yelled, and started to reverse,

but Maximus was in the way. In Maximus' cockpit Sammy looked very confused. Jimmy hit the Cabcom.

"What's the matter?" said Sammy.

"Cabbie's freaking out! Can you back up?" Maximus's reversing light pinged on, but before they could even move, Cabbie tried to turn in the cramped space. "Cabbie, no!" Jimmy shouted. He could see there was no room to turn, and the robot's nose swung into the wall beside them. Instead of the expected crunch of metal, however, there was a sharp click, and the carving that Cabbie had bumped into – a gruesome image of a man with a pierced nose, tongue and lips – sank into the wall like a light switch being turned on.

No light appeared, though. Jimmy turned in his seat as he heard a scraping sound, and saw a giant stone slowly roll into place at the end of the tunnel, cutting off the corridor just behind Maximus. The two boys and two robots were now well and truly stuck in the tight space. And the tunnel was silent, except for the sound of hissing from the pit at the end.

"We are trapped?" said Sammy.

"Yes," said Jimmy. "It would seem so."

"Sorry," said Cabbie. "I just really *don't* like snakes."

"Don't worry, Cabbie," said Jimmy, patting the dashboard. "We'll find a way of getting out. We've got plenty of time."

As soon as he said the words, Jimmy knew he would regret them. First he heard a squeaking noise, like an ancient mechanism turning after years of neglect. Then the corridor was filled with the sound of stone scraping on stone. Jimmy looked to the side of the corridor and saw what he had feared. The carvings on either side were getting closer.

The walls were closing in!

CHAPTER TWELVE
Time to Escape

It was happening slowly, but Jimmy was sure of it. The grey stone walls on either side of the corridor were getting closer and closer.

"Sammy! It's a booby trap! It must be to protect the temple. We've got to get out!"

Maximus said something on the Cabcom, and Sammy translated. "Maximus has calculated that we have five minutes at the current speed before the robots start to get crushed," he said. He sounded surprisingly calm.

"What do we do?" said Jimmy. He was starting to panic himself now.

"Whoever built this would have put in an emergency stop button to stop themselves being crushed," Sammy told him. "We just have to find it."

He got out of his cockpit and Maximus flooded the small space with light. Jimmy followed, and they desperately searched the walls for a button of some sort, pressing carvings and lumps and bumps in the hope that it was the switch that would stop the stone walls sliding towards them.

A minute or so later they had been down the whole corridor.

"There are no more carvings to try," said Jimmy.

"Don't be so sure," said Sammy. Jimmy looked up, and tried to see what Sammy was looking at. He was staring at the viper pit, and to a small ledge on the other side. On the wall there was a carving of a puma, sealing the corridor off in a dead end. Its nose seemed to glisten in the light. *It could be the button we need to stop us being crushed*, thought Jimmy.

"Y-you can't be serious," said Jimmy. "There's no way we can get past the pit."

"Oh, I don't like this at all," muttered Cabbie.

Sammy shrugged. "It's worth a try."

Before Jimmy could stop him, Sammy had taken a run up, and launched himself across the pit. His feet flew just a metre above the hissing, wriggling snakes. A huge viper snapped upwards, its deadly fangs slicing the air just centimetres from Sammy's feet. Sammy calmly landed softly on the other side of the pit, and with a hiss the snake sank back down, spitting angrily.

"See? It's no big deal." Sammy reached out and touched the puma's nose.

There was a loud click and the walls which were closing in shuddered to a stop.

"Nice one, Sammy. You did i—" But Jimmy didn't get a chance to finish his sentence as a second loud click echoed around the temple. Then the walls began to move again, but this time they were moving twice as fast.

"Erm, that was not part of plan," Sammy said uncertainly. He gave the nose another tap, but the button was now locked in place and it wouldn't budge.

"Sammy, it didn't work. Get back over, quick!"

Sammy launched himself across the pit again, but the small ledge didn't give him much of a run up. He flew through the air above the angry snakes, but this time his foot landed on the very edge of the pit, and he slipped. His foot slid down towards the snakes, and he gave a small yelp as he realized what was happening. Jimmy dived forward, reaching for Sammy's hand. For a moment he thought he wasn't going to make it, and he would see his friend tumble into a shimmering pit of poisonous reptiles. But his sweaty palm found Sammy's and the two boys gripped each other desperately.

"Hold on," Jimmy said through gritted teeth. He could feel his hand slipping, and see Sammy's eyes widening in panic. Jimmy thrust his free hand forward and desperately reached for Sammy's other arm. He managed to grasp onto his other wrist, getting a better hold on him.

For a moment, they dangled above the viper pit, Sammy's legs kicking madly as he tried to gain a foothold somewhere. The snakes below hissed and spat, and the giant viper jumped up once again. This time it sunk its teeth deep into Sammy's trainer.

"Aaaah!" said Sammy in desperation. He shook his foot, causing the snake to hiss even more dangerously.

He shook it again, harder this time, and the huge snake finally let go.

Jimmy gripped tighter, and used the weight of his own body to pull his friend to safety. They both collapsed onto the floor.

"Are you OK," Jimmy asked urgently. "You've been bitten."

"I am fine," Sammy replied, inspecting his shoe. "The snake bit only the shoe and not my foot. But we will both be dead if we not get out of here fast."

"It's no good," said Jimmy. "We've tried everything I can think of."

Sammy actually laughed. "Is this the famous British spirit? I thought you chaps never surrendered?"

Jimmy was stunned. He couldn't believe that this boy who was always so super-serious could laugh at a time like this. The moment that his father wasn't around all the time issuing orders, Sammy became a different person. He was funny, more confident, daring, and very quick-thinking.

Sammy seemed to stare off into the distance for a moment. He appeared calm – in spite of the solid walls which were threatening to crush them like a vice. Then, after a moment he shouted, "Wait! I see something." He yelled an instruction to Maximus in Arabic, and the hoverbot killed the lights, plunging them into darkness. "Look."

Jimmy wasn't sure where he should look in the pitch black, but it soon became clear. High up on the wall at the end of the corridor was a tiny speck of light.

"Daylight!" he shouted. "We can escape!"

"Yes, if only we could open that hole wide enough to drive out."

Jimmy had an idea. "I've got just the thing!"

Maximus lit up the corridor again, and Jimmy hurriedly searched around inside Cabbie. He came out holding something smooth, silvery and rocket-shaped. It was the nitro-blaster which had been knocked off his side earlier.

"It's blasting time!"

"Will it blow us an escape route?" said Sammy, his face full of hope.

"It should do. I didn't use all of the fuel in this blaster earlier on."

Maximus said something in Arabic, and Jimmy was pretty sure it wasn't good news.

"He says we have two minutes," translated Sammy. "Let's do it."

Jimmy stood on Sammy's shoulders, steadying himself against the wall. He attached the nitro-blaster to it near the small chunk of sunlight. He used some strong sticky tape that Grandpa had left in Cabbie's boot. Jimmy was fairly certain that it was how Grandpa fixed Cabbie together.

"Will it do it?" Sammy asked.

"I don't see why not," said Jimmy. "Grandpa's got a knack for blowing things up. He won't let me down now."

"One minute!" said Sammy. They looked at the side walls, which were frighteningly close. They were already touching the rubber air cushions which kept Maximus hovering, and even the super-cool Egyptian robot sounded worried as he gave a countdown to the moment when they would be squeezed like a lemon.

"Thirty seconds!" Sammy took cover in Maximus, and Jimmy dived into Cabbie.

"Cabbie, will this work?" he whispered.

"I've patched into the nitro-blaster's remote sensor so that I can detonate from here. It should make short work of that wall, but there is no way to tell if it was damaged in the fall or not," said Cabbie. "There's only one way to find out."

"Ten! Nine! Eight! Seven!"

"Here we go!" Jimmy pressed the button that was flashing on Cabbie's dashboard and dived for cover. There was a horrible split-second pause when Jimmy thought the blaster wasn't going to work, and then—

KABOOM!

The nitro-blaster activated, and the explosion sprayed chunks of rock and dust down onto them. Without giving the dust a chance to settle, Jimmy floored the accelerator and hurtled straight for where he hoped a hole was.

"Wooooaaaahhh," he yelled as he felt Cabbie flying over the rubble, and the next thing he knew he was being blinded by bright light of a jungle clearing.

As Jimmy's eyes adjusted to the daylight, he heard the loud whirring of a giant fan and then Maximus emerged from the dark depths of the underground temple. And just in the nick of time. Moments later there was another rumbling noise from inside, and with a great big thud the two walls clashed together, blocking the exit they had just made with the nitro-blaster.

"Woo-hoo!" cheered Jimmy, jumping out of his cab. "That was amazing!"

Sammy got out of his cockpit. "We high-five now?"

"Yes we do!" They slapped their hands together. "Sammy, I never would have made it out of there without you. If you hadn't kept calm and noticed that gap, Cabbie and I would be flat as a cream cracker by now."

"But we would have been stuck if you had not packed volatile major explosives." Sammy grinned. "This is teamwork, yes?"

Just then there was a crackle and a hiss from inside Cabbie. The Cabcom had started to work again, now it was back out in the open air where it could receive a signal from the RoboNet satellite. The two boys squeezed into Cabbie. Grandpa's worried, sweating, white-moustached face popped onto the screen.

"There you are! Oh, thank goodness! And Sammy too! Are you safe?"

"We are now!" grinned Jimmy.

"Although my bodywork has seen better days!" chipped in Cabbie.

Jimmy launched into an explanation of what had happened, and where they had been for the last few hours. Sammy enthusiastically helped to fill in the exciting parts. When they had finished, Grandpa wiped his brow and looked exhausted, like he'd been through the whole ordeal himself.

"Well I'm just glad you're both OK. I've been worried sick."

"Please, Mr Roberts," said Sammy. "Is my father there?"

Grandpa looked around and turned back to the camera, a bit embarrassed. "He, er ... he went off to get dinner."

Sammy looked shocked. "He is not worried?"

"He sounded more angry actually," said Grandpa. "He kept muttering 'ghabi' or something. I'll tell him what happened and that you're all right."

Sammy went quiet.

"Are you at the overnight camp? Save us some dinner!" Jimmy joked, trying to change the subject to cheer his friend up.

Grandpa shook his head sadly. "Sorry, Jimmy lad – race rules state you must start on day two from the exact same spot that you stopped at. That means that you'll have to stay put overnight."

Jimmy and Sammy exchanged a look.

"Right here? In the jungle?" Sammy asked.

"In the dark? With the creepy-crawlies? Jimmy said, trying to sound brave.

"Don't worry, boys, you'll be fine," said Grandpa. "Just whatever you do, don't—"

The screen popped and went dead. Grandpa's face disappeared, leaving Sammy and Jimmy alone in the dark with the sound of the jungle growing louder and louder and louder…

CHAPTER THIRTEEN
Campfire Tales

"We're alone," said Jimmy. "In the jungle."

"With no camping supplies," said Sammy.

"But lots of wild animals and insects," said Cabbie.

The three of them crept closer to each other. Maximus muttered something in Arabic.

"What did he say?"

"He said, 'Pull yourselves together, you big soft pussycats,'" said Sammy. "He's got a point."

Cabbie seemed to take offence at this. "That's easy for you to say, you big hunk of metal!" he said. "I've had a rubbish day, and it's— aaaaagh!" Something had fallen on Cabbie from the trees above, something long and thin. He started driving forwards and backwards, trying to shake it off. "Anaconda! Get it off! These things could swallow me whole!"

With a snap, he flicked open his bonnet and the long thing was tossed high into the floor before landing just a few metres away. Sammy picked up the thin trailing vine that had fallen from the tree canopy. Above them, some monkeys seemed to laugh, and the group below couldn't help but laugh too.

Sammy's quick thinking kicked in and he organized them both into setting up camp. After searching through Cabbie's boot they found a few useful things. There was a large tent canopy that Grandpa had packed weeks ago in case he needed to fix Cabbie in the rain. There were two sleeping bags and bottles of water, packed for just such an emergency, along with a packet of Grandpa's favourite marshmallows, and a fruit salad from *That's Shallot!*

Sammy didn't have any emergency gear, apart from a sticking plaster in his back pocket. He explained that his father did not believe in emergencies, and preferred to keep Maximus's weight low in order to make him faster. Jimmy happily shared his things with

Sammy and they set up the tent, stretching it between Maximus and some trees as shelter in case it rained – and, more importantly, in case the cheeky monkeys decided to throw anything else down at them. As it grew dark, they sat on upturned logs and used one of Maximus's pryo-booster engines to light a fire so that they could toast their marshmallows.

Cabbie had parked alongside Maximus, and the two were soon chatting happily away in Arabic, Cabbie using his in-built translation chip. Jimmy couldn't be sure, but he thought that Cabbie was boring Maximus with stories of celebrities he had given a ride to when he had been a regular taxi.

"You and Cabbie seem to get along together well. You talk like friends," said Sammy.

Jimmy shrugged. "I suppose we do. Grandpa programmed him, so I suppose Cabbie's just like him. We disagree sometimes though. What about you and Maximus?"

Sammy looked down suddenly at his marshmallow, which was dripping hot pink goo onto the leafy jungle floor. "Father says you should not be friends with a robot," he said sadly. "I should be master, not friend."

Jimmy swigged at a bottle of water. "Sammy, do you *like* being a robot racer?"

Sammy did not answer for a long while. "It has always been my father's dream for me to be Robot Races champion," he said at last.

"And what about you?" Jimmy asked.

"It is my dream too," said Sammy quickly. "But ... Father knows what I should do in a race, and I do not."

He looked sad, as though the whole race was getting on top of him. Jimmy tried to cheer him up.

"I think you know exactly what you need to do. You knew how to get us out of the temple, didn't you? And how to set up the camp?" Sammy nodded. "And you enjoyed every second!"

Sammy laughed. "Yes, very much."

"So when you haven't got your dad shouting orders at you, you're a brilliant racer."

Sammy let Jimmy's words sink in. "Father only cares about the race." He took a bite of his hot marshmallow and raised the stick he had used to toast it like a sword. "I will show him. I can be a real racer. I am not 'ghabi'." He sat up straight and tall, determined. He caught Jimmy frowning. "It means 'stupid'. We will see who is stupid when I race tomorrow!"

After a few more marshmallows, Sammy seemed much happier. They talked for a long time, and Jimmy found him to be completely different to the quiet person he had seen at the press conference in Cairo. The boy he shared a tent with now was loud, energetic and knew an impressive amount of terrible knock-knock jokes.

Before long the efforts of the day began to catch up with the boys and they decided to settle down for the night. Jimmy hopped into his sleeping bag and curled up on Cabbie's back seat.

"Good night, Sammy," he called across the space. Sammy was laid out in Maximus's cockpit.

"Good night, Jimmy. Sleep well."

"Good night, Maximus," said Jimmy.

"*Tisbah ala kheir!*" called the robot.

"He says good night," translated Cabbie.

"Good night, Cabbie."

"Night!"

Jimmy closed his eyes and was just drifting off to sleep when—

"Er ... Jimmy?"

"Yes, Cabbie?" Jimmy yawned.

"Could you throw a couple more logs on the fire? It's pretty dark now and I wouldn't want you to get too cold and—"

Jimmy grinned. "Cabbie, do you want the fire to keep snakes away?"

There was a long, embarrassed silence before Cabbie spoke again. "Yes, please."

Jimmy put more wood on the fire and made sure that it wouldn't set the trees around them alight. Then he climbed back into Cabbie and fell asleep, the sounds of the rainforest all around them.

After a few hours of sleep, Jimmy was woken by bright sunlight streaming through Cabbie's windows. He rubbed his eyes and sat up. Outside the jungle was waking up too. Birds were singing their morning songs, small animals were collecting their breakfast of chittering bugs, and the cheeky monkeys in the trees above were howling a wake-up call, telling him to get out of bed. It was a clear and bright morning, and Jimmy felt refreshed and ready for anything.

"Morning, Jimmy!" said Cabbie energetically. "It's a brand-new day and that means only one thing!"

"We've got some racing to do!" said Jimmy, pumped up with energy. He leaped out of his sleeping bag and out into the jungle. Sammy was just getting out of Maximus, stretching and yawning.

"Good morning!" said Jimmy. "Did you sleep well?"

"Yes, thank you, but I thought I heard something in the night. It sounded like someone saying 'Slither off!'"

"That was me, sorry," said Cabbie. "I thought I saw a snake, but it turned out to be my windscreen wiper."

"Don't you mean, windscreen *viper*." Sammy laughed.

Jimmy and Sammy tidied up their camp and arranged the start time for the next leg of the race with the Robot Races officials through the Cabcom. Because Cabbie and Maximus had come off the official track in an accident, they had to make their way directly to the official track, go through the luxury camp where everyone else had slept and carry on with the race from there. They had much more ground to cover than the other racers, but all they could do was try their best.

Grandpa popped up on the screen after the officials went away. "Jimmy? Did you have a good night?"

"Yeah, sort of," said Jimmy. It had been fun, but he hadn't got much sleep, and he still had Sammy's knock-knock jokes ringing around his head.

"Omar is going mad over here. He says he can't contact Samir."

"Oh, yeah. Tell him the Cabcom was damaged in a freak accident," said Jimmy. He looked over to Sammy, who grinned as he pointed to the pink marshmallow oozing out of his Cabcom.

Then suddenly a ten-second countdown appeared on Jimmy's Cabcom to start the second leg of the race.

"Cabbie and Maximus, are you ready?" said the voice of Joshua Johnson, the robot co-ordinator, over the speakers.

"Born ready!" said Cabbie.

"Then you are good to go in five..."

Cabbie revved his engine.

"Four..."

Maximus's turbo rotors span, readying themselves.

"Three..."

Jimmy looked over and gave a nod to Sammy, to say 'good luck'.

"Two..."

Sammy gave a salute back and turned his attention to the race.

"One! Go, go, GO!" shouted Joshua Johnson.

In a flurry of leaves and mud, Cabbie was off! To Jimmy's surprise, Maximus was hot on their tail, a smiling Sammy at the controls. It looked like Jimmy was right – without his dad yelling at him, Sammy was a great racer. Sammy was taking corners at high speed, throwing Maximus around the track in daring manoeuvres that his father would never approve of. He was achieving spectacular results, and from the look on his face Sammy was having the time of his life!

They soon found their way back onto the official track, and within just a few minutes both robots were hurtling into the main camp with its rope bridges and treetop cabins. Grandpa was waiting at the pit stop, and he waved at Jimmy to pull in. The rest of the teams had had all night to patch up, repair, reprogram and refuel their robots, but for Grandpa it was a race against the clock. As Cabbie pulled in, race officials stood over him with a stopwatch and clipboard in their hands. Joshua Johnson stood with them.

"Crikey, you've been in the wars, haven't you?" said Grandpa as he saw the state of Cabbie, but there was no time to chat. He placed his steaming mug of tea on top of Cabbie's roof and got to work.

Grandpa whizzed around the car, refuelling and checking tyres. The other crews, which were made up of mini service robots and technicians in white overalls, looked on at Grandpa as he zipped around the robot. He stuck a fuel nozzle in the side of the car, quickly re-inflated the tyres, muttering about not having time to change them completely, and threw a banana into the driver's seat, which Jimmy accepted gratefully. He wrenched off the broken fender and kicked a dented side panel until it popped out. He then squirted a bottle of water over the windscreen to clean it, and banged the roof to show he was finished. He just had time to pull the fuel nozzle out of the side of the robot and grab his mug of tea from the roof before Jimmy sped away, his wheels spinning.

Jimmy glanced in his rear-view mirror as he tore away – he could see Grandpa fall into a nearby chair, exhausted, while Sammy's pit crew were still working on Maximus feverishly.

"Well done, Grandpa!" Jimmy laughed.

Driving away from the pits, the jungle closed in around the track again. Up ahead, he could see the trees growing thicker, and the light below the tree canopies was so dark that Jimmy wasn't sure that he would be able to pick out the right way to go.

"Hey, Cabbie, you remember Horace said he had a better navigation system than you? Well, I think it's time to put it to the test."

"Received and understood, Jimmy!" said the chirpy robot. "Calculating route now."

There was a series of blips and beeps, and a map popped up on the screen, a red line indicating the best route to take. "This will guide us through this thick forest. Hold on tight, pay attention, and I'll talk you through the bends," said Cabbie. "If you follow what I say exactly, we can do this at top speed."

"OK," said Jimmy, slightly nervous. "Let's do it!" He focused, tightening his grip on the steering wheel as the trees grew closer, listening out for Cabbie's navigation instructions. As the trees closed in on him, he instinctively braked.

"No, maintain your speed!" said Cabbie, and Jimmy put his foot back on the accelerator. "In ten metres, turn thirty degrees left. Now!"

Jimmy did so, narrowly missing a giant tree that must have been there for hundreds of years.

"Slight right, past that ant hill on the left."

Jimmy winced as he brushed the ant hill slightly with a wing mirror. He wanted to shut his eyes, but then he'd definitely crash. Cabbie kept shouting instructions, and Jimmy followed them to the nearest centimetre, trusting the robot's directions and his own reactions to get them through. They were still on the official track, which was marked by glowing markers on trees and posts, but Cabbie was taking a risky route, clinging to the edge of the track to keep the speed up, and flying over bumps in the road rather than going round them.

"Left! Right! Forty-five degrees west! Hairpin

bend!" yelled Cabbie, branches whizzing past them, leaves and insects splatting against the windscreen. "Chicane coming up!"

Jimmy braced himself as he came to the tight S-bend. He threw the steering wheel to the left and right, manoeuvring through the little glowing posts. He came out of the obstacle and Cabbie shouted at him once more as they headed into a sharp bend that Jimmy hadn't noticed.

"Eeek!" said Jimmy as they missed a tree by millimetres. He held his breath as they skimmed over the top of a large, deep, dark puddle. He didn't speak until they were clear of the trees and back onto a nice, clear mud track.

Jimmy breathed a sigh of relief that they had made it through, and concentrated on the route ahead. They turned a corner and saw the other competitors only a few hundred metres in front of them.

"We've caught up!" said Jimmy. "If we can get in front of this lot, we could still win the race!"

"That's the spirit!" cheered Cabbie.

Jimmy was excited at the thought of whizzing past Horace, but his smile faded slightly when he saw why the other robots had slowed down. The track took them over the top of an area that looked like a yellow lake.

"Quicksand!" he gasped. The other robots were being careful – they knew that if they slipped off the track, they would sink like stones and be out of the race for good.

Monster was at the back of the group, following the others down a safe route at the centre of the track. Missy had obviously lost a few places since Jimmy and Cabbie had made their daring overtake the day before.

"Get out of the way!" said Cabbie. Jimmy steered them to the left, and tried to push past Monster, but Missy must have seen them coming. She steered left too, blocking the way. Jimmy immediately steered right, trying to overtake on the other side, but Monster followed, blocking the way past again.

"Well, if that's the way you want to play it..." muttered Jimmy. He looked directly ahead and quickly guessed the height of the monster truck in front of him. "We can just make it!"

"Make what?" said Cabbie.

"If we can't go round her, we'll have to go under," Jimmy replied. And with that he hit a button on the steering wheel. There was a whirring noise and Cabbie's suspension lowered, making the whole car hunch down lower to the road. Jimmy floored the accelerator and powered right beneath Monster's chassis. They passed huge wheels on either side. The sound was deafening and the vibration from the enormous engine above him made Jimmy's teeth chatter together. For just a second he felt like he was trapped in a giant hairdryer.

But then they sped between the front tyres of Monster and back into the daylight ... and fourth place!

Just a few hundred metres ahead was Lightning.

"Let's see if we can get past Her Highness!" said Jimmy. He put on a burst of speed and soon he was almost touching the back of Kako's robobike.

Jimmy glanced down at the Cabcom, checking the map to assess his progress. Two dots were blinking side by side – Cabbie and Lightning. Just then he saw his opportunity.

"Here we go!" he said. He kept his speed and

waved at Kako. She smiled back, looking over at him. Suddenly the track came to a bend. Kako had been caught off guard and had to slow down to go round it safely. Jimmy had seen the bend ahead, and he was ready. He roared through it, keeping his speed the same and overtaking Lightning. Once in front, he powered away to extend the gap between him and the Japanese princess.

"That's my boy," came Grandpa's voice over the Cabcom. "You're making mincemeat of them, Jimmy."

"Thanks, Grandpa. Cabbie, how far ahead is the next racer?"

"Just under half a mile, Jimmy. You should be able to see Dug at the end of this straight."

Sure enough Jimmy caught just a glimpse of Chip's huge racer up ahead. But he knew that Dug would be even trickier to pass than the last two.

"Just under fifteen miles to go. That's not much racing time, Jimmy. If we want to beat Smelly Pelly, we'll need to make this pass double quick."

"I know, I know. We never make things easy for ourselves, do we?" Cabbie jokily sighed. Jimmy knew he was enjoying every minute.

Jimmy manoeuvred Cabbie to the far right of the track as he sped up towards the rear bumper of the giant diggerbot. As he expected, Chip blocked the way past. Jimmy swerved to the left, but was blocked. Then he tried to pass to the right once more. Again he was blocked by the American.

Now I've got you where I want you, Jimmy thought. He wrenched the steering wheel to the left again, but only for a second. When Dug moved to block the way on the left, Jimmy quickly whipped the steering wheel to the right again and overtook in the large space that the digger had left.

Cabbie's engine roared and they zipped by an astonished Chip. "Ha ha!" laughed Cabbie. "Nice move!"

Just at that moment Horace's sneering face appeared on the Cabcom. "Been having fun with Scabbie, have you, Jimmy? Well, now you've finished messing around with the amateurs I'll show you how us pros do it."

Jimmy and Cabbie were in second place now, close enough to see Zoom's shiny black bodywork in front. Jimmy accelerated and they pulled alongside Zoom.

Horace glanced at them from his cab. "Back again, Jimmy? You never learn, do you?"

Cabbie was about to overtake, when the familiar jets of red-hot flames shot out from the centre of Zoom's wheels.

"Yowser!" screamed Cabbie, and pulled to the side, but he kept his speed. He had singed the outside of his tyres, and Jimmy again smelt the nasty smell of burning rubber.

Horace laughed as he pressed the button again, and the flames shot out even further this time. It forced Cabbie to the very edge of the track, closer and closer to the huge pool of quicksand on his left. His tyres screeched as they rubbed against the edge of the track. Jimmy looked, and saw the quicksand waiting to grab hold of him and pull him down into its depths.

"No way, Horace! Not again!" shouted Jimmy.

CHAPTER FOURTEEN
Race to the Finish Line

Jimmy's face turned red with anger. He gritted his teeth and roughly slammed the steering wheel with a fist.

"Ow! Watch it!" said Cabbie.

Jimmy didn't say anything. He was so cross that for a moment he thought about simply ramming into Zoom. "No," he said to himself quickly. "That's how *he'd* race. It's not my style."

Suddenly the roar of Dug's engine was upon them as the track widened and Chip took the opportunity to steer the digger robot alongside the other two. In their efforts to outdo each other, Jimmy and Horace had given Chip a chance to catch up.

Dug hurtled along between Cabbie and Zoom. Whereas the flames from Zoom's wheels had burned the rubber on Cabbie's tyres, they had no effect on Dug's tough steel body and his thick tractor-like tyres. He glanced over at Jimmy, giving a smile and a wink before his face appeared on the Cabcom, next to Horace's.

"Hey, guys! Mind if I join the party?" he said, a glint of wickedness in his eye. "This one's for you, Horace!" He pressed a button on his dashboard and – *whomp!* – there was an explosion of smoke from Dug's rear end. The smoke billowed out, creating a cloud of thick fog around Zoom and Horace, making it impossible for them to see.

Horace yelled out in terror as Zoom veered wildly.

Jimmy smiled. After what Horace had done to Chip and Dug in the last race, they deserved to get their own back. The fog was as thick as Grandpa's home-made porridge, and Jimmy could hear Horace panicking over the Cabcom.

"Aaaargh! Activate the laser guidance system!" Horace squealed like a little girl.

A grid of lasers shot out from Zoom's nose, but the smoke was so thick that they couldn't cut through it. A series of confused bleeps came from Zoom, and the computer-assisted steering program almost screamed as it lost its way. Zoom hit the edge of the track and the engine roared as his wheels spun madly. The sleek black robot launched over the edge, sliding down into the quicksand with a final *splosh*!

"Aaagh! Deploy emergency life-saving apparatus!" said Horace to Zoom.

"Life-saving apparatus is situated below the pilot's seat," said the cool, calm tones of Zoom. After a moment of fumbling below him, Horace came back on the screen.

"Rope? *Rope*? Is that the best you can do? I want my money back from NASA!"

"Er – Jimmy?" called Cabbie. "QUICKSAND, DEAD AHEAD!"

"Uh-oh," said Jimmy as he saw what Cabbie was talking about. In front of them the road was sunk into the lake of quicksand. The track ended and picked up again about a hundred metres later, leaving no other way to finish the race. And Cabbie was just seconds away from the yellow pool of sandy sludge.

"Slow down!" said Cabbie.

Jimmy glanced at the rest of the racers behind him, and quickly hatched a plan. "No! Quick, Cabbie, release the EFD!"

"Pardon?"

"Activate the Emergency Floatation Device!"

"The *what?*"

Jimmy sighed. "The rubber dinghy! Inflate the dinghy, quick!" he shouted.

"Oh, right!" said Cabbie. "Why didn't you say so?" With a noise like a hundred whoopee cushions, a rubber skirt unfurled around Cabbie, and a canister of compressed air inflated the device within seconds. "Jimmy? Did you know you're speeding up?" said Cabbie's worried voice.

"Yup," smiled Jimmy.

"We're going to hit the quicksand at full speed! Slow down!"

Jimmy kept his foot on the pedal and patted Cabbie's steering wheel. "It's OK, I know what I'm doing. I think..."

They raced along the track to where it sank into

the sand, and hit the quicksand with a loud *slosh!* But instead of sinking, Cabbie glided across the pool as the dinghy kept them from sinking into the deadly gloop. It was almost peaceful, sliding across the sand. The engine was quiet and Jimmy just had to wait to hit the track on the other side.

He looked behind him and found the rest of the competitors squealing to a stop, unable to make the jump to the other side. Everyone, that is, except Sammy and Maximus, whose hovercraft cushion was perfect for this sort of situation. They headed onto the quicksand without a moment's hesitation, and travelled just as easily as they did on the road.

Jimmy had timed his sail across the quicksand perfectly. He was just losing speed when the road appeared again, and he was able to drive off onto the path.

"That was *so* lucky!" said Cabbie.

"Nah!" Jimmy chuckled. "It was exactly how I planned it."

They were in first place! Jimmy looked back to see Maximus emerging from the quicksand and following at speed. He could also just make out the rest of the competitors on the other side. Chip was using Dug's giant robotic arm to swing from overhead trees across the pool like a metal monkey. Missy had over-inflated Monster's massive tyres so that she could float across, and Princess Kako had reversed Lightning back a long way, and it looked like she was going to attempt a giant one-hundred-metre jump using her turbo-thrusters. There was no time to see how they got on, though, as Maximus was hot on their tail.

"Let's go, go, *go!*" said Jimmy.

However friendly Sammy and Jimmy had become, Jimmy knew that their friendship would have to be put aside until they crossed the finish line. They were true robot racers and neither was prepared to give an inch. Maximus pulled alongside Cabbie.

"How far until the finish line?" shouted Jimmy above the noise of the straining engine.

"Not long!" said Cabbie. "Keep your eye on the road, though. We've got a few more corners to go yet."

The first corner came almost immediately, and Jimmy skidded round it in a high gear. Maximus was right by his side, the hovercraft's back end drifting out as he made the turn. They were just centimetres apart. Jimmy glanced over to see Sammy hunched over his controls, concentrating on the race. Next came a hairpin bend, which the two robots raced round as fast as their drivers dared.

Then the finish line came into sight. Jimmy could see the crowds at the finish line now, roaring their support. It was clear that Sammy was going to give up on first place – and neither was he!

"If only we still had our nitro-blasters," muttered Jimmy. "Come on, Cabbie, just a bit faster!"

"This is all we've got!" the robot shot back. "It's going to be tight!"

Jimmy held his breath. Time seemed to slow down for the last few seconds of the race. He was aware of the crowds in the stand, waving their flags in slow motion. He could see the journalists waiting up ahead, and he saw Sammy beside him, gripping the wheel tight as he too raced towards the finish line. The sound seemed to drop away and all Jimmy could hear was the muffled cheers of the fans and the tinny whirr of the engine.

Cabbie and Maximus flew past the finishing post,

past Lord Leadpipe, who was waving his chequered flag furiously. But it was several seconds before Jimmy let himself breathe again. The cameras around the grandstand flashed, and the sound returned to normal as the crowd let out an almighty cheer. It was the loudest thing Jimmy had ever heard.

Cabbie and Maximus both slowed to a stop and Jimmy leaped out onto the track, where Sammy was already waiting, his helmet in his hands. They looked around.

"Who won?" the boys said together, but the race officials just shrugged at them. No one knew who had crossed the line first.

An electronic leaderboard by the side of the stands flashed, and Jimmy and Sammy looked over.

"Seeking official race results," said a computer voice. Jimmy felt too nervous to talk, but nodded 'good luck' to Sammy. The crowd was silent.

"Photo evidence inconclusive," said the computer again. "No winner was identified. Now seeking results from advanced laser finish line technology."

Jimmy was willing the computer to come up with the right result as he focused on the leader board.

"The results have now been found," said the computer finally.

"And?" muttered Sammy.

"*And?*" whispered Jimmy.

There was one more tantalizing moment before the display changed. Suddenly the crowd erupted.

"First Place – a tie! Jimmy and Cabbie *and* Sammy and Maximus!"

Sammy and Jimmy stared at each other in disbelief. The photo finish on the screen confirmed it – they had crossed at exactly the same time! A message ran over the bottom of the screen:

For the first time in Robot Races history
a tie has been awarded
for the title of first place.
Well done, Jimmy and Sammy!

Jimmy ran to Sammy and shook his hand. The Egyptian smiled and pulled him into a great big bear hug. They heard the crowd chanting their names.

"Sam-my! Jim-my! Sam-my! Jim-my!"

"I think they're calling for you!" said Jimmy.

"I think they want both of us!" corrected Sammy. They both ran over to the grandstand and waved to the crowd in celebration, giving high-fives and shaking hands.

The other racers came in past the finish line and slowed to a stop. Chip came in next, followed by Missy and Monster, who were covered in sand. Kako came in fifth, and did not look happy about it.

The leader board flashed up the results and last on the screen was Horace and Zoom, with a red 'DNF' next to their names – *Did Not Finish*. It was over ten minutes later before the safetybots finally trundled in, dragging a sandy-looking Zoom. The safetybots stopped by Jimmy for a moment and Horace did his best not to catch Jimmy's eye – his face was red with barely-contained anger.

Jimmy peered into Zoom's cockpit and noticed it looked a little bare. "Where's the laser guidance system you added?"

"If you must know, it fell off and sank in the quicksand," spat Horace. "And I intend to complain to Lord Leadpipe himself about the unsafe track and deadly traps, not to mention the sabotage by that

American! The whole race should be discounted!"

His whining trailed off as the truck moved on, taking Zoom off to the pits to be fixed and cleaned out. Jimmy started to walk away towards the pits.

"Hey!" said a voice behind him. "Where do you think you're going?"

It was Joshua Johnson, with a big smile on his face. He grabbed Jimmy and led him and Sammy over to a small stage, where they were both pushed onto the top of the winner's podium. It had only been built for one winner, but Jimmy and Sammy both squeezed on happily.

The officials gave them both a giant bottle of lemonade. Jimmy grinned at Sammy and knew exactly what to do. He popped the cork from the top of his bottle and started shaking it up. Sammy copied him, then both boys sprayed the fizzy drink everywhere! The crowd cheered as they turned the bottles on the fans and journalists who were snapping their photos.

With the last bit left in his bottle, Jimmy hopped down from the podium and approached his racer.

"You look a bit dirty, Cabbie. Fancy a wash?" he said mischievously.

"Don't you dare!" shouted the robot, but Jimmy had already shaken the bottle again. The lemonade fizzed over the top and sprayed over Cabbie's bonnet, the robot protesting the whole time. Joshua Johnson grabbed them again for more photos on the podium before he would allow them to leave.

Jimmy could hardly hear himself think with the crowds shouting his name, and he didn't even notice Grandpa running towards him. He was lifted off the ground in his second huge hug of the day.

"That's my boy!" laughed Grandpa, his wiry arms gripping Jimmy tight. Jimmy looked over, and saw the stern face of Omar Bahur approaching, a scowl on his face as usual. He faced Sammy, and extended a hand for a very business-like handshake. Sammy gave his hand too, and looked shocked when his father broke out into a grin and gathered him up into a bear hug instead.

"Samir, my child, you were extraordinary! Your first Robot Races win! A father has never been so proud!" They released each other and Sammy smiled, looking confused and embarrassed by his father's unusual behaviour. "You must forgive me. I know how much of a – what is this word? – *bully* I have been. I must be a better father in the future."

"Quite right too!" muttered Grandpa under his breath.

"You are remarkable! Quick-thinking and brave!" continued Omar. "Such an intelligent boy!"

"Yes. I must get it from Mother," Sammy joked. The crowd around him laughed.

"I'd still be at the bottom of a hole if it weren't for Sammy!" said Jimmy. They were about to shake hands for the cameras when two men in green suits and smelling slightly of cabbage barged in and took Grandpa and Jimmy off to one side. A photographer approached, snapping pictures.

"Jimmy, it's a great pleasure to meet you finally!" said the first man, shaking his hand very hard indeed. "I'm Felix Crump from *That's Shallot!*. This is my business partner Jasper Sprout. I trust our little gift came in handy?"

A TV camera was now being pushed in Jimmy's face. "Erm ... yes. The Carrot Vision was a life-saver," said Jimmy, a bit taken aback by the two strange men.

"Of course!" Felix Crump grinned at the camera.

"Our carrots are packed full of goodness and really do make you see in the dark!" he said, addressing the camera like a man in a cheesy advert. "And that's why we're giving you a lifetime supply of carrots! What do you say to that, Jimmy?"

"Er…"

"Overjoyed, you say? You're welcome! And it's all thanks to *That's Shallot!*: Your cheaper way to five-a-day!"

Grandpa managed to pull Jimmy away. "How are you feeling, Jimmy?" he said.

"A bit overwhelmed, to be honest. Everyone's congratulating me."

"Get used to it, boy! This is what it's like to be a winner!" Grandpa smiled and pointed up to the big screen, which now showed the results of the two races overall. Jimmy felt like he was in some sort of bizarre dream as the announcer read the results and the crowd cheered as each name was mentioned. They came to the top of the leader board.

"And let's hear it for Jimmy Roberts and his robot Cabbie as they climb to the top of the leader board. First place! Great job!"

The crowd cheered and screamed his name as Felix and Jasper from *That's Shallot!* hoisted him onto their shoulders in celebration.

"Yes," said Jimmy to himself. "I could get used to this…"

CHAPTER FIFTEEN
Congratulations to the Winner

It was a long time before the crowds calmed down and Jimmy was placed safely back onto the ground. And even longer before the journalists and TV crews had stopped shouting out questions like:

"How does it feel to share first place?"

"What's the secret to a good race?"

"Have you got anything you can tell the folks back home?"

Jimmy didn't know which to answer first, but luckily he saw that someone was coming to take control of the situation. Through the crowd of cameras and the tangle of wires came a familiar face.

Bet Bristle from Robo TV battled her way through the other journalists, knocking them out of the way with her elbows. "Well done, boys!" she said with a smile that silenced the rest of the journalists. "Tell me, we lost you on the tracking system for a while yesterday, and neither of your teams could contact you. What happened?"

Jimmy took the lead in the interview, and explained about their daring adventure.

Bet looked exhausted at the end of the tale and turned to Sammy. "Samir," she said, "you've been typically quiet throughout all of this. How did you cope with this ordeal?"

Sammy looked at the crowd, and did not answer straight away. Instead, he took a pair of sunglasses out of his coat pocket and put them on, looking like an ice-cool pop star.

He shrugged. "I wasn't frightened at all," he said.

Bet tried to get more out of him, but he refused to answer any more questions. Jimmy raised an eyebrow at his new friend, and when the journalists had moved on to talk to the other competitors, Sammy looked over the top of his shades and smiled.

"I have an image to think of," he said. "It might be fun to be the cool, silent guy!"

Jimmy shook his head in disbelief as Sammy walked off to sign some autographs.

With the attention of the world finally off him, Jimmy was about to make his way to the pits to see how Grandpa and Cabbie were doing when he heard a voice call out, "Our young winner!" It was Lord Leadpipe, his monocle glinting in the light of the sunshine. "Congratulations, Master Roberts. Good race, eh? You're turning into quite the champion!"

"Thank you." Jimmy felt his cheeks turning red.

"Let's see if this pack of hungry photographers would like a photo of me with the winners, hmm?" said Lord Leadpipe with a chuckle. He started to lead them towards the press pit, where some paparazzi turned and began to snap away at them.

Jimmy felt a hand clamp down on his shoulder, stopping him. "No more photographs, Ludwick," said Grandpa, appearing by his side. "The boy's tired."

Leadpipe seemed startled by Grandpa's sudden appearance. "Well, quite. I suppose you have a lot of debriefing to go through. Team talks, as it were."

Grandpa nodded, fixing Lord Leadpipe with a silent stare. Only when Leadpipe broke the stare and turned around to leave did Grandpa say anything.

"That's the thing with Jimmy and me," he said. "We *are* a team. We're loyal, and we stick together."

Lord Leadpipe turned on his heel to face Grandpa again, but before he could say anything in response, someone shouted, "There he is!"

Jimmy turned to see Mr Pelly marching up to Leadpipe, looking like he was going to explode with anger. He was almost glad to see him, and pleased he had distracted Grandpa and Leadpipe from their confrontation. Horace trailed after his dad, covered in mud and sand. He looked like one of the Amazonian beasts that Jimmy had seen on the walls of the underground temple.

"Ludwick! I want a word with you about track safety! My boy could have been killed!" he said. "And what's worse is that my robot is now ruined! There's sand everywhere!"

Lord Leadpipe waved his hand in a 'pish-nonsense' sort of way. "Pelly, you'll have to take this up with the track stewards," he said dismissively. "I have a very important announcement to make!"

He took to the stage in the centre of the race compound to the sound of a cheering crowd. His face appeared everywhere at once, on every TV screen, including two huge ones the size of billboards. It was even projected onto the entire side of the Leadpipe Industries airship which hovered high above their heads, and appeared across the world on millions of screens.

"Big-head," muttered Grandpa.

"Robot Races fans!" boomed Lord Leadpipe. "Our racers have defeated the Rainforest Rampage, but there are tougher tasks yet to come. I can tell you that the next race will be enthralling, exciting and of course, unexpected. And I will be introducing a very special twist!"

The crowd oohh-ed like they were watching a pantomime.

"But that, my friends, is all I will say for now." Lord Leadpipe flashed a grin at the TV cameras, then pointed his special gold-tipped walking cane at the sky. He pressed a button on the handle, and crackling electricity shot from it into the clouds above, where fireworks flashed and banged, lighting the jungle up with bright reds and yellows. It looked like the sky was on fire, and the crowd oohh-ed again.

As the familiar sound of the Robot Races theme tune kicked in and the audience clapped along to the beat, Lord Leadpipe turned back to the TV cameras. "Don't forget! Stay tuned for the next instalment of the engine revving, rough-and-ready, rip-roaring Robot Races, coming soon!"

"I wonder what's he got up his sleeve this time?" said Grandpa.

"Well, whatever it is, we'll be ready for it!" said Jimmy.

ROBOT RACES
RESULTS TABLE

RACE 2: RAINFOREST RAMPAGE

Race Position	Racer	Robot	Points
1	Jimmy	Cabbie	18
2-	Kako	Lightning	12
2-	Chip	Dug	12
4	Sammy	Maximus	10
5-	Missy	Monster	6
5-	Horace	Zoom	6

Look out for more **ROBOT RACES** adventures!

Jimmy Roberts loves watching the Robot Races, where drivers and their super-smart talking robots compete. When a new race for kids is announced, Jimmy is desperate to join in. There's only one hitch – he'll never be able to afford a robot. All Jimmy can do is watch while his worst enemy, Horace Pelly, boasts about the robot NASA are building him.

But then Jimmy's grandpa reveals that he hasn't always been a taxi driver. In fact, he might be the only person who can help – by turning his battered old taxicab into a real-life robot!

Will Jimmy and his robot Cabbie ever be able to keep up with the competition?

Jimmy and Cabbie are off again, and this time there are three fiendishly difficult Arctic routes to choose from. Cabbie's been fitted with lots of things to keep them toasty warm, but Jimmy's sneaky arch-enemy Horace and his robot Zoom have got a flamethrower ... and they're not afraid to use it!

Are Jimmy and Cabbie's chances of winning melting fast?

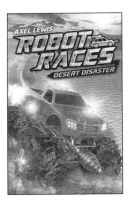

The adventure through the sweltering Sahara desert is a race with no track! Missy and her huge robot, Monster, are used to racing in the Australian outback, but even they are stumped when the robots and their racers have to solve clues to find the right direction. It will take brains as well as gadgets to reach the finish line!

Can Jimmy and Cabbie surf the sand dunes and finish first?

For more exciting books from brilliant
authors, follow the fox!
www.curious-fox.com